Born to Dream

Born to Dream

The Journey of Arvind AI

HARSHVARDHAN RAO

Srishti
PUBLISHERS & DISTRIBUTORS

Srishti Publishers & Distributors
A unit of AJR Publishing LLP
212A, Peacock Lane
Shahpur Jat, New Delhi – 110 049
editorial@srishtipublishers.com

First published by
Srishti Publishers & Distributors in 2022

10 9 8 7 6 5 4 3 2 1

This is a work of fiction. The characters, places, organisations and events described in this book are either a work of the author's imagination or have been used fictitiously. Any resemblance to people, living or dead, places, events, communities or organisations is purely coincidental.

The author asserts the moral right to be identified as the author of this work.

To Dada Ji (Late Beni Madhav Bhatt)
And Aakka (Late Manorama Devi).

This book is affectionately dedicated.

Acknowledgements

To my caring, supporting, and loving wife, Megha. My deepest gratitude. Your support and love when the times get rough are much appreciated. You provided all the comfort and relief when you looked after household activities while I completed my work. My heartfelt thanks.

Finally, lots of love to my sons Vihaan and Rishvik.

Prologue

The auditorium was packed. Finally, it was time for the most admired speaker to take the stage. Even though he was second in line to speak, he was the most awaited guest in that gathering. Almost everyone in the hall was there to listen to his story.

When it was time for his speech, the light was dimmed and the noise in the hall slowly faded away. After a few seconds, when it was completely dark, a spotlight fell at the centre of the stage and on the mic. All eyes beamed at the mic. Arvind walked briskly onto the stage and stood under the spotlight. He warmly greeted the audience by folding his hands and smiled radiantly at them.

The audience was applauding enthusiastically, the noise decibel breaching all limits. Some people whistled and shouted his name. Slowly all the audience started to chant the name, "A.I", "A.I", "A.I"!

Arvind was not nervous at all. Instead, he was calm and composed. His personality was brimming with confidence and aura. His head was held high with pride and conviction. Arvind waved his hand with a gesture to everyone to settle down.

After a few minutes, everyone became silent. They were ready to listen to Arvind Ingle, A.I.

Arvind came near the mic and said, "Hello everyone! Would you like to have tea?"

This time, the audience cheered even more loudly. Each one of them stood up again and said "Yes". They knew they were looking at the person who used to sell tea in the college canteen earlier. However, through his hard work and dedication, he had turned around his life and transformed himself into a billionaire.

Starting off as a canteen boy, he became a business tycoon and was recognized as A.I. in the business world.

How did he transform from Arvind Ingle to A.I.?

The audience was ready to listen to his inspiring story.

"I am thankful to my mother, god, and each one of you. Without your love and blessings, I would not be here. I owe a lot to my mother, and the only way I can feel her around me is by keeping my family name Ingle. I got this family name from her." Arvind looked up and said, "Sarasvati Ingle, I hope your son is making you proud!"

The auditorium reverberated with incessant clapping. The people were enamoured by the love and respect that Arvind carried in his heart for his mother. It was so deep that he used his mother's family name as his surname.

.

Arvind took out the mic from the stand and held it in his hand. The next few hours belonged to him to tell the world his incredible story – his journey of becoming AI.

1

The Canteen Boy

Autumn was slowly taking over and the monsoon season was at its trailing end. Mussoorie was feeling a flurry of moderately cold air in October.

Maharani Janaki Kunwar College of Engineering, called MJK popularly, was full of students and staff. Ajit Trivedi, the owner of MJK canteen, was as busy as a bee. He desperately needed a helping hand. Luckily, someone was coming to help him and he was eagerly waiting for him.

Trivedi had a tough time getting a dependable person for his canteen. Youngsters were not interested in working in the college canteen as most of them used to migrate to Delhi from the close villages of Uttar Pradesh. Trivedi was adamant that he would only bring someone from his village. He did not want to bring a stranger onboard to run his canteen business. As a result, his options were limited, so he had to wait for a long time.

Around 7 p.m., a bus coming from a remote village of Uttar Pradesh stopped at the last stop, Picture Palace Bus Station. I was twenty-one years old back then, totally unaware of what was in store for me in the new city. I got down from the bus with a heavy trunk. I vividly remember that chilly, cold October night.

I put my hand inside the jacket and pulled out a piece of paper that had an address written on it. I looked around and went to a nearby shop. I showed the shopkeeper the address, to which he gave me the direction to Trivedi's house. Shivering, I made my way to my new destination.

•

Trivedi was staying alone. He had a flat-mate who had gone back to his village and showed no sign of returning. He had cited the reason that his father got a heart attack and he had to go. Now, Trivedi had to pay the full rent of the room from his pocket. It was an extra burden which he had been bearing for a couple of months.

Trivedi looked outside the window in anticipation. His eyes were stuck on the road, hoping to see someone coming towards his house. His long wait to find a helping hand was finally about to end.

When I reached Trivedi's house and knocked on the door, he rushed to open it. He saw a young boy, shivering in that chilly night. The boy was wearing a thin jacket, which was not enough to protect him from the chilly winters of Mussoorie, standing with a heavy trunk. He looked at me and smiled.

"You should have known how cold nights are in Mussoorie, especially at this time of the year. Come, Arvind, come inside quickly!"

I walked inside the room. I was quiet and waited for Trivedi's instructions. Trivedi pointed me to the corner, to keep my trunk. The house was small, just like a matchbox; it had one room that included an open kitchen and an attached bathroom. He showed me a cot and a small wardrobe where I could keep my belongings. The room size was not more than ten square feet.

Trivedi asked me to sit. He went to make tea to warm me up. While making tea, he talked about the water supply and gas connection. He even showed the kitchen setup. There were few small jars of spices, grains, flour, a small stove and a couple of utensils. He asked me if I could cook food, to which I nodded my head. After having tea, I helped him with cooking. I had brought my plate, spoon and bowl. That day, dinner was ready earlier than the usual time. I was indeed the helping hand that Trivedi had long been waiting for!

"Have you come to Mussoorie for the first time?" Trivedi asked me while lying in bed. He was perhaps looking at the ceiling.

"Yes, I have never left my village since I was born," I replied.

"That would be a difficult decision to make? What did your mother feel about it? It would be the first time she would be alone in the house," Trivedi turned towards me and asked curiously.

"Aai, my mother, is a tough lady. She married my father, who was not from her caste. That decision was taken purely from her heart. But the worst came when she was thrown out of the village, at a stage where she was eight months pregnant. She could have died. My father left his job at Ratnagiri and took her back to his village. She got all the love and care in my father's house. Aai was lucky that the village people accepted her, even though she was not from their caste. They continued to love and respect her even when my father died, when I was barely one year old.

" Now, I have left her for this canteen job. I know she will not take dinner today, but I believe that she will understand and live her life, eventually. Without me!" I took a deep breath and closed my eyes, thinking about Aai.

"A tough lady! Now you are here! Make your Aai proud by showing commitment and honesty towards your work. And yes, your Aai also told me that you would be appearing for your final exams of Master's in Psychology in December. Good that your distance learning has one exam centre here in Mussoorie.

"So, after work, you can study. I also hope that you get a better job someday, so that you are able to leave this canteen job and do something bigger in life," Trivedi said with a smile.

It was perhaps a spell of his comforting words or my tiring journey, due to which I drifted into a pleasant sleep.

•

It was a bright, sunny morning, and the temperature was moderate. It was less cold compared to last night. I was comfortable in my light clothing, and the breeze was making me feel cozy.

We started early to go to college. Trivedi explained to me about the nitty-gritty of the canteen business on the way. The job was not complicated. Most of the time, people ordered tea, and my work was to serve them before it turned cold, especially during winter time.

Trivedi also told me that canteen time got extended till midnight during exam days, as students who studied late at night came to the canteen to have tea. Inside the canteen kitchen, there was a big copper vessel in which tea was prepared. That big vessel never got unloaded from the burner once it was set on fire in the morning.

I kept that copper vessel atop the stove, poured water, tea leaves, and tea masala. Trivedi taught me that once the aroma of tea leaves starts to come out nicely, then I was to add milk to it. That tea masala was Trivedi's secret recipe, which he kept in a big plastic jar. He filled it up at the start of every month.

I was instructed to take that masala in an optimum quantity, for which he had a measuring spoon so that it would last for a month and not get over before that. In the canteen, we also sold samosas and other curry puffs, which Trivedi looked after. He told me to take care of tea and ensure that the utensil never overburns from inside. He told me that he used the words 'Chai half, Chai full' and attached a number with it. Mostly, students came to the counter to collect it. But sometimes, we had to serve at the table. Whenever that was needed, he would tell me the exact table location and I would just follow his instructions.

My first day was not as complicated as I had imagined it to be. Even though it was busy, Trivedi helped me to ensure that the students didn't get disappointed with the service.

While walking back to our house, Trivedi said, "I think the crowd will increase now in our canteen."

"Why is that?" I asked out of curiosity, to which he said jokingly, "A tall, young and good-looking boy like you will now give a tough time to the handsome students. Girls will come to the canteen more frequently now. And following them will be the boys." He laughed. I blushed at his compliment and continued walking.

•

When I reached home, I asked Trivedi if he could lend me his phone to call Aai. When I left the village, Aai told me not to buy a phone. She knew that if I bought a phone, I would keep calling her every now and then, and it would disturb my work. But I knew for a fact that she really missed me a lot.

A mother needs a strong heart to send her child away so that her child achieves something meaningful in his life.

My Aai was always selfless and looked after everyone in the village, expecting nothing in return. Aai taught me that we should live our life with a lot of grace and dignity.

Excitedly, I called Aai. I told her everything that had happened since I reached Mussoorie, about Trivedi and my new job. While talking to her, I felt that she did her best to hide the sadness that she was experiencing since I was not around. I also stopped myself from asking her about how she was feeling at home, without me.

Towards the end of the conversation, she said, "Aru, it's good that you have started to earn and look after yourself at this young age. Always remember that no work is small. You know Chajju, who used to clean our house? Think about that smile on his face! No matter how dirty the kitchen floor used to be, he performed his responsibility with full sincerity. Learn from Chajju and be happy with what you do. Your canteen job is only the first step. You have to grow and achieve bigger milestones. Always try to find what makes you happy and strive to reach that goal. Help Trivedi by taking more initiative. And most importantly, take care of yourself."

"I will do that, Aai," I said and ended the call.

Later that night, after our dinner, I asked Trivedi about the rent of the house. Trivedi hesitated a lot and told me that he would take care of it, but I insisted.

Finally, after much convincing, he agreed to deduct it from my salary every month. I was happy to share the load.

•

Sometimes, I also had to deliver tea to the staff room, principal's cabin and meeting room. That day, while I was preparing the tea, a peon came at the counter and told Trivedi to make twelve cups of tea for a meeting being held in the staff room around 10 a.m.

Trivedi instructed me to run with the tea to the meeting room before it turned cold. I was nervous. For me, it was like a relay race. Sharp at 10 a.m., I put the tea cups in the stand, filled it, and ran towards the staff room. I got there within a few minutes. When I reached the door, I looked at the tea; the vapours were still coming out. I was glad to see that it was still hot.

I knocked on the door and went in. The professors saw me panting; they asked me to sit down and catch my breath. But I continued to serve the tea to each of the staff members. While I was placing the cup in front of each staff, I heard them talking about an event that was supposed to happen after fifteen days. They were talking about an important person, perhaps a motivational speaker, who was visiting the college.

MJK was a prestigious college in Mussoorie. Few alumni held key posts in the ministry of the state and even at the national level. The meeting was held to plan necessary arrangements for his visit.

2

Cold Tea

As days went by, I started to notice the unique relationship that existed between Trivedi and the students. Trivedi called each of them by name. He was aware of what the preferences of his customers were. His trick was simple; call people by their name. That way, he was able to establish an amiable relationship with his customers.

"Trivedi, can I say something? Please don't mind! I have noticed that you are biased towards students when they borrow things from the canteen. Why is that?" I asked out of nervousness.

"I know why you are asking this, Aru. Look, customers are like your god. But even god doesn't have money sometimes. You can't upset your customers, but then, you also can't give them freebies. It's against work ethics. Right?" Trivedi took a pause and continued, "So, the best option is to give them freedom until a certain level of debt is collected, based on their capacity to pay. The students in this college come from different backgrounds. You have to be a little considerate about their economic situation."

"But how do you know about their financial status?" I asked curiously.

Trivedi laughed and said, "It's simple; talk to them as much as you can. And always remember their names. It is a great way to cultivate personal relationships."

"I have a lot to learn from you, Trivedi," I chuckled.

"And one more thing, if you will build personal relationships with them, they will come to the canteen more, which means they will spend more," he said and smiled.

•

One day, a group of students came to the canteen and sat at the table. They aggressively asked Trivedi to deliver some snacks and tea.

This was unusual! I felt that something was not right! Trivedi looked at them and waved, signalling them that he would bring the tea to them.

I was baffled that even though they were so uncouth, Trivedi still entertained them. Trivedi placed some curry puff and samosas on a plate and asked me to make four cups of tea. Once it was ready, he picked it up and started to go near them.

But after walking a few steps, he turned back, handed that plate, and told me to serve them.

Hesitantly, I took the plate from him, but was not comfortable serving. Trivedi sensed my discomfort, but didn't say a word. I went and kept the plate on the table. Each one of them gave me a strange look. While I was going back to the counter, one of them shouted, "Hey you, come back!"

I stopped and looked at Trivedi. He looked at me for a moment and then started counting the money at the cash counter. I turned and went to them.

One of them said, "This tea is so cold! Why don't you give me a straw to drink it!" he giggled. All the students at the table started laughing loudly.

Feeling nervous, I picked the cup, turned back and looked at Trivedi. It was apparent that he was ignoring me.

I went back into the kitchen and poured the boiling tea into the cup. I served them again and when I turned around to come to the counter, the same boy shouted, this time in a loud voice, "This tea is cold; why are you serving us cold tea?" I went back and picked the cup. To my surprise, it was actually cold. I was totally baffled now.

Trivedi was watching everything, and surprisingly, he never came and asked me about what happened. When I went back to deliver tea for the fourth time, Trivedi asked me to add two more cups to the plate. So, I made six cups of tea and went to them.

Trivedi followed me and I kept all six cups on the table. This time, Trivedi also sat at the table and asked me to sit with him. I followed his instructions. Trivedi stared at one of the students and said, "Let's have tea together. Shall I join you? Don't worry about the ledger. We will talk about it later."

Everyone was quiet. They looked at each other in surprise. Now, even after a few minutes, the tea was still hot. Each of them gave a glaring look at me and took their cup. Trivedi and I also took our tea. Each one of them finished the tea and ate their snacks quietly. They paid the cash to Trivedi on the table itself and left.

I asked Trivedi, "What was going on?"

Trivedi knew the situation which I was facing. It was natural for me to get nervous. But, he deliberately put me in front of them so that he could see how I tackled the situation.

"Why did the tea always turn cold even when I served it hot?" I asked.

Trivedi took a pause and said, "Did you notice the level of tea in the cup? Did it remain the same when you served them and when they called to tell you that it was cold?"

"No, I never noticed."

"So, you didn't believe in yourself. You didn't think that you did the *right thing* and they could be wrong. You served them hot tea; it turns cold in a few seconds. How? Unless, someone *made it cold*. Whenever you served them tea and turned back, they poured a little water in it. And in this weather, the room temperature is less than 20 degrees Celsius so, it turned cold immediately. If you had noticed that the tea level was a little higher than usual when they were calling you again and again, you would have spotted it."

I was lost in thoughts. "What else could I have done?"

"Aru, you could have been smarter and sat with them to see what they were up to. Like I did! When we were in front of them, they couldn't pour water in the tea and it remained hot. They didn't have any option but to drink it and pay the bill." Trivedi smiled and looked at me.

"Why did they do this to me? I don't even know them," I asked, surprised.

"Why not! You are in college, a new bird. Why would they spare you?" he giggled and further added, "But unless you stand firm in front of them and give them the room to play with you, this will happen. If there is a problem, sit with them and look at it together. If the problem is real, then you all will find a solution. And if it's fabricated, then you will discover a loophole," Trivedi said and stood up. I tapped my shoulder and walked towards the counter.

Why didn't I see that the tea was more than what I had brought to them? I was still lost in thoughts.

While I was at the counter, thinking about what had just happened, I saw one girl sitting at a table alone. She was there with her book, but she hardly flipped pages while the whole event was unfolding. Instead, she kept the pen between her teeth and was looking at me furtively, hiding behind the book.

After a while, a girl came to the counter to pay the bill. I took the money and gave the change back. She looked at me for a couple of a second and left the counter.

What if something like this happens again and Trivedi is not around to help me? Will I be able to deal with it?

•

At night, I called Aai and told her about everything that had happened in the canteen. After I finished my story, she told me, "Aru, what do you want to do now? Do you want to come back and leave everything?"

"Aai, I am not sure what to do now? Do you think I would be able to handle such situations again? Please tell me!"

She replied, "From now on Aru, it's not important what I think about you? The more important thing is how you perceive yourself. This will shape your future. No matter what choice you make, keep in mind that you are just twenty-one! You have a long way to go. Remember, I will not be around to look after you always!"

I understood what she meant. I told her that I will stay and face whatever obstacles come my way.

"Whenever you take any decision in your life, stay firm on it. No matter what happens. Don't worry about how it will turn out, always hang in there! If you manage to do that, you will always succeed."

I listened to every word attentively. She continued, "I can see that you are talking to me more frequently using Trivedi's phone. How are you going to pay him back?"

"Shall I pay him after every call?" I asked.

"Do one thing, make a small piggy bank. And whenever you call me, see how many minutes you have spoken to me for. Then deposit that many coins in that piggy bank. Say, if you called me and we spoke for two minutes, then put a two-rupee coin in that box. After the end of each month, give him all the money. This way, you will be disciplined about your time and will be able to pay Trivedi back."

I loved the idea. After the call finished, I pulled out a small empty spice box and cleaned it up. That day, I deposited five one-rupee coins and kept the box near the bedside.

3

A New Feeling

The preparations for the upcoming event were in full swing in college. I could hear the college students incessantly talking about it in the canteen. Probably some of them were even volunteering in the event.

Trivedi told me that it's the annual event which had been taking place for more than twenty years now. He told me that they call this event 'Yuva Utsav'. It was a three-day event which included many exciting programmes. He emphasised that this time, a special guest would be coming to the Yuva Utsav.

Slowly, I started enjoying working in the canteen. I was adapting myself to the environment and slowly connecting with people. But, the ease with which Trivedi interacted with them was commendable. It was a long way for me to go.

While I was in the canteen, the same girl came in. Again with her books, and she was sitting alone. She opened the books on the table and started flipping the pages, pen between her teeth. After sometime, she came to the counter and asked, "Tea please, one full cup."

I went in and came back with the cup of tea. She picked up the cup and went towards her table. After walking a few steps, she turned back and looked at me. Suddenly, she asked, "Why is it cold?"

Upon hearing that statement, my heart rate spiked and my hand turned cold. Whatever happened yesterday flashed in front of me. She took a pause and laughed. Then, she said, "I am just joking, dear!"

A few minutes later, I gazed around the tables and stopped at the table where that girl was sitting. She was not there anymore. I tried to remember whether she had paid the money for the tea or not. While I was thinking about the bill, I saw a notebook which she had forgotten on the table. I swiftly went over and picked it up. I flipped the pages to see her name, but there was no name written on it. Only a few pages had scribbles. I brought the notebook with me and kept it at the counter, hoping that she would come back soon.

But she didn't turn up. My eyes were looking at each girl to see if she was the one, but no luck. Later that day, when we were returning to our house, Trivedi asked me, "Hey Aru, why were you looking at everyone in the canteen today? Did you expect someone?"

"Yeah, a girl who ordered tea today! I forgot whether she paid the bill or not. When I tried to look for her, she was not at her table. However, she left this notebook." I showed the notebook to Trivedi. He looked at it and said, "Don't worry, if she visits the canteen daily, she will come tomorrow too."

•

When we reached home, I saw someone standing outside our gate. Trivedi squinted his eyes and looked at the man who was apparently waiting for him. He slowly murmured, "Shukla".

I looked at Trivedi as he hurriedly walked towards him. I followed him and saw Trivedi hugging that man and then shaking his hand. Trivedi introduced me to Ratikant Shukla, his room-mate who had left Mussoorie a couple of months back due to a family emergency.

"Why are you here after so long, Shukla?"

"Let's talk inside." He said and we entered the house.

Shukla told Trivedi that he needed the room for some time and would find a place for himself soon. Although Trivedi said that the room was full as I had joined him, he insisted. So, it was decided that until Shukla found his own place, he would stay with us. We decided to move the cots away and put the bedding on the floor in such a way that there was more space for us. Even though the room was more packed, but we needed to help Shukla.

After dinner, Shukla told us everything. He used to work with a rich and successful businessman, Ranjit Singhania, in Mussoorie. Ranjit trusted Shukla a lot and treated him as one of his close associates. He had diverse businesses under the name of

Singhania Industries. They were into the carpet business and also in agriculture, mostly growing potatoes and exporting it out of Mussoorie.

Ranjit was the only child in the Sighania household. Despite that, he was not a spoiled brat. He worked hard, even more than his father, and had a bigger contribution in bringing his company to the top. He had an only son, Rahul, whom he loved dearly.

A couple of months back, Shukla's father suffered a heart attack, so he had to go back. Back then, Ranjit gave a good amount of money to Shukla for the treatment of his father. Shukla owed Ranjit a lot. He got all the respect and money that he needed from an employer.

Recently, Shukla got a call from Ranjit to come to Mussoorie. Ranjit had some urgent work for him. Shukla did not ask any questions. His only mission was to serve his boss.

•

The next day, the girl whom I was looking for came into the canteen. Surprisingly, she came with her two friends. She came to the counter and asked for some tea and samosas. I thought of asking her about the money she didn't pay last time, but I did not know how to initiate the conversation. The samosas were still getting fried, so I asked her to wait for a few minutes. After a few minutes, the samosas were ready and I put them on a plate with three cups of tea. She picked up the plate and left.

Trivedi came out from the kitchen and I told him about the girl. He told me to go and speak to her.

I went to her table and stood behind her. She was busy talking to her friends. I stood there for a while before I said, "Excuse me."

She turned back, looked at me for a few seconds, and said, "Yes?"

"I want to tell you something," I said in a shaky voice.

"Yes, tell me!" She frowned and asked curiously.

"Actually, I am sorry to say it this way, but you didn't pay the last bill for one cup of tea."

She laughed out loud, "For which one, the cold tea or hot tea?"

"The cold, sorry, I mean... the hot tea," I fumbled.

Her friends nudged her. "Leave that poor boy! Don't tease him."

She looked at me again and said, "I always pay the bill. Which one you are talking about?"

I quickly ran away from the sight and went back to the counter. I took out the notebook and went to her.

"The day you left this notebook!"

She took the notebook from me and said, "Thank you for the notebook, but I paid the bill."

"No, you didn't pay the bill!" I replied in a louder voice.

"What proof do you have?" she asked.

"I don't have any, but I remember you didn't pay. See, my mother told me to be honest with my work. I can't lose money; I owe Trivedi this money. Can you please pay the bill?"

She smiled and said, "Okay I will pay, now go!"

I came back to the counter and waited for her to finish the tea and samosas. After an hour, they got up and came to the counter; she paid the money and went out. When I counted the money, I noticed she still hadn't paid for one cup of tea. I went to her and asked, "You still didn't pay the money for the tea."

She looked at me and said, "Are you crazy?"

"Whatever you call me, but I need my money."

She looked inside her purse and said, "I don't have change right now. I will leave by 5 p.m." She pointed to a scooter standing in the parking. "You can come by that time and take your money."

I nodded and got back to work. I waited till 5 p.m. I went and waited for her near the scooter. She came and gave me a fifty-rupees note.

"But, I don't have change, ma'am."

"You can give it to me tomorrow."

She took the scooter out from the stand. While sitting on the scooter, she asked, "Are you always like this? Chasing someone till you get your money back?"

"I am sorry about this, but this is my first job. And my Aai told me that when you make any decision in life, don't turn back. This time I had decided that I had to take my money back," I told her, keeping my head down and looking at the scooter's stand.

"Who is Aai?" she asked.

"My mother, I call her Aai," I replied.

"I liked what she said. What else did your Aai tell you?" she asked.

"She tells me a lot of valuable lessons."

"You are mama's boy, haan!" She giggled. Then, she took a pause, and continued, "I want to hear more about your mother; I might also learn something valuable. Let me come to the canteen tomorrow and we will talk. Are you supposed to talk during working hours?"

"Okay!" I was shy and continued, "I think I can manage. I will ask Trivedi if he can allow me to talk to someone while on duty."

"See you tomorrow, then!"

My heart skipped a few beats when she said that. Strangely, I felt very exhilarated. It was indeed a new feeling.

4

Restless Heart

The students were gearing up for Yuva Utsav. There were banners and flags scattered across the college campus. There was excitement everywhere as students flocked to set up stalls and tents.

I was in the canteen alone since Trivedi had some urgent work in the morning. So, he wanted me to handle the work. Since morning, things had been rather busy. I was so preoccupied that I didn't even remember the girl whom I had to return the change to. And she also didn't come to the counter to get her money back.

Finally, in the afternoon, I saw her sitting at a table with her books and pen between her teeth. I took out the change from the cash counter and went to her table. She was so engrossed in her book that she didn't even notice my presence.

"Excuse me, ma'am!"

She looked at me and asked, "Yes?"

"Here's the change I owe you," I replied.

She took the money and said, "Okay, thanks!" and continued reading.

"It's not good to keep the pen between your teeth," I murmured.

"Why? Will I break my teeth?"

"My Aai says that you will not receive knowledge if you disrespect your pen," I said.

She shook her head in disappointment and said, "I disagree and thank you."

I realised that she didn't want to be disturbed, so I started walking back to the counter. While I was going, she shouted, "Please, one tea, full cup."

I nodded my head and went into the kitchen. Quietly, I kept the tea near the corner of the table, close to her books and went back to the counter. She didn't realize that the cup was there. So, while flipping the pages of the book, she unknowingly hit the cup and it fell on the floor, I swiftly ran to the table to help her. She looked at me and said in a loud voice, "Didn't your Aai tell you to inform the person when you place a hot cup close to them!"

"I am sorry! I thought you were busy with your studies, so I didn't disturb you. Let me clean this up."

I quickly went into the kitchen, brought a floor mop and cleaned all the broken glass pieces. She was intently staring at me. I cleaned up the floor and got a fresh cup of tea for her.

I kept the tea near her and said, "Please, take this tea."

She looked at the cup and said, "Thanks!"

I went to the counter, picked up a magazine to read. Suddenly, I heard the noise of someone tapping at the counter with their knuckles. It was the same girl, standing in front of me.

"Hey, listen! I am sorry, I was rude. I didn't mean to disrespect you," she spoke gently.

I shook my head to tell her that it was okay. She continued, "And I am very sorry for what I said about your mother. She is a great lady!"

"It's fine. It happens sometimes," I replied.

"So, do you also like to study?"

"Yes. In fact, I am pursuing my Master's in Psychology from distance learning."

"That sounds interesting. Tell me more about it. Let's have tea together. Come, join me!"

Trivedi was back from his work now, so I asked him. Since he didn't mind, I came out of the kitchen with two cups of tea and went to the table where she was sitting. At the beginning of the conversation, I was quiet, but later, the rapport started to build up. We talked till evening. Trivedi watched us, but he did not interrupt. She left the table around 5 p.m., at her usual time.

When I came back to the counter, Trivedi looked at me and asked, "Who was she?"

"I didn't ask her name. So silly of me!"

Trivedi smiled and told me to count the cash and tally it to the total sales which were written in the notebook. Even though I was counting the cash, my mind was wandering to the moments

I had spent with that girl. This was the first time I had talked to someone for so long.

Why I was thinking about it so much? It was just a regular interaction.

Trivedi saw that I was day-dreaming, but didn't interrupt me. Though later, he came to me and said, "Why are you taking so much time to count a few entries? Wake up!"

"Sorry, let me do the final counting," I replied and focused on the task at hand.

While we were walking back home, both of us were silent. Trivedi sensed that something was not right. "Do you want to work in the canteen for your whole life, Aru? What will you do once you finish your Master's?"

I didn't have any answer to his question. Trivedi continued, "See Aru, Master's in Psychology is no less than the Bachelor's degree students pursue from here. You have the same potential as them. While you are here, focus on your work and when you get home, manage your studies. Whatever you earn here, save it to spend it later on yourself when you are in the city, looking for a job."

"But what job can I get?" I asked.

"If you try harder, you will certainly get a better one than a canteen boy."

I nodded. After a pause, he told me, "The girl that you were talking with today is a scholar. If you want to know her name, just go near the staff room. Outside, there is a big board. Her name is in the list of toppers. She studies hard, which is why she is such a brilliant student. But in your case, you have to work harder, both in your studies and your work."

That night, I was up till late, thinking about whatever Trivedi had said to me. The last thought on my mind before I slept was why Shukla hadn't turned up after he went to Ranjit's house. We still didn't know the reason why Ranjit had called Shukla back to Mussoorie.

•

I worked sincerely at the canteen in the days to come. Surprisingly, I didn't see that girl again in the canteen. I often crossed the staff room to give tea, but I didn't check her name. Gradually, I started to spend more time on my studies. Mussoorie was getting colder with every passing day.

One day, when I went to buy groceries and other snacks for the canteen, I saw a very interesting ad on a board:

Learn how to speak English in two weeks in American accent. Job guarantee at a call center. Talk with confidence. Earn more by talking like a gentleman.

I was intrigued. Just below the board, there were also some pamphlets lying around. I picked one and kept it in my pocket.

After a few days, that girl finally came to the canteen. The moment I saw her, my heartbeat spiked, my hands turned cold, and restlessness gripped me.

She walked directly at the counter towards me and said, "I need your help!"

5

Lions and Orcas

Singhania Industries was going through troubled waters in the carpet business. Ranjit Singhania was busy fixing some issues related to the export of the carpets to other states. One of the reasons was that his labour union was planning to take industrial action through protest. They were unhappy because the pay had not been increased in the last few years.

Ranjit had decided to offer health benefits instead of increasing their pay. He was the first one to provide those benefits in private firms, but slowly, other players also started adopting a similar strategy to capture the market and labour force. This brought in more competition.

Till now, he was the undisputed leader among all the industrialists in the state. But slowly, his grip was weakening. He was desperate to get hold of the rein more firmly now. So he organised a dinner party to plan for the future.

•

In the garden, everyone was sitting around the bonfire. Ranjit's party consisted of the elite group of the town. The other local businessmen aspired to become a part of this group, but not everyone was privileged.

Ranjit stood up and looked around at each of them. He said, "Thanks to all of you for joining me for dinner. We all know why we have gathered here. Unions were always there; some of you were not even born when I was in this business. So, I understand how their needs change over a period of time.

"When there was an endemic of pneumococcal infection in the region, I started to issue health insurance, even to daily wagers. They worshipped Singhania Industries. But now, when the fear of pneumonia has gone, they don't worry about their health insurance anymore. Since you guys came into the region, the insurance policy was common. But now, when the focus has shifted towards monetary gain, they don't worry about health anymore. Let's not cut each other's throats by paying them more. There should be a consensus, a common rule and loyalty that bind us together." Ranjit paused, finished his drink, handed over the empty glass to the servant standing near him, and continued.

"But, it looks like some of our friends here are creating their own rules. They are innovative. So, my question is, why don't you share the idea with everyone here? Let's all follow the same rule and play the same game." He stopped and sat on his chair.

Everyone was murmuring. Then, someone said from the other side of the bonfire, "Why should we all follow the rules? We should be independent. People should be given the freedom to play their hand in the game as per their wishes, with no boundaries."

Ranjit could not see his face clearly. So, he stood up and walked towards him. He was Brajesh Thakur. His father Jagan Thakur was in the timber business. Even though he was a man of few words, he had become very close to Ranjit as he was dependable and competent.

Jagan had died two years ago in a road accident, just after he joined Ranjit's elite club. Brajesh believed that someone from the business circle had killed him. His needle of suspicion was always on Ranjit.

Ranjit reached Brajesh's chair, "Do you know about a pride, my son? It is a group of lions who hunt in a group. Sometimes, they are surrounded by a pack of hyenas that come together and take away their part of the food. But together, they can counter the hyenas and stay strong."

Brajesh looked at Ranjit and said in a lower voice, "Do you know about pod, Ranjit? These are a group of orcas' whales. They also hunt in a group, more active than lions."

"Let's stick together, Ranjit and Brajesh. Let's not argue about who is right. And Brajesh, Ranjit has been here for a long time. Don't forget that he introduced your father to us. Now, you have grown from where you were. It doesn't make sense to change the rules. So sit down, both of you!" Deepak Bhandari said.

Ranjit said, "I have heard that people are paying more to the workers. I am fine with this. Let us agree on the wages that we all will follow. There is no point in pulling the trigger at each other."

Everyone in the meeting agreed to the fact that standard wages should be allocated to the workers. It was decided that Ranjit would speak to the labour union and buy some more time. By then, new wages will be rolled out by Singhania Industries and others will follow it.

After dinner, Brajesh came to Ranjit and said, "The problem with orcas is that when they are hungry, they are ready to even kill the weakest among them. I am sure we understand that killing our own people will not do any good. I haven't found any evidence on who killed my father. Till then, my eyes are on you."

Ranjit replied to Brajesh, "You know how the pride grows? The lion kills other lioness's cubs to gain their territory. If I had to gain anything from your business, you know who the cub here is. Think about it! I have always supported Jagan, even when debtors crushed his pocket. I even sponsored your education at Yale. So be careful and don't play dirty games with me. Remember, I am running Singhania Industries since a decade, even before you were born. Revise the worker's wages and let us stay together."

•

The next day, Ranjit met the worker's union at his office to present his offer. The union knew how influential Ranjit was, so they agreed to accept the offer.

Shukla was in Ranjit's office, waiting for him outside his cabin. After the meeting, Ranjit came out of his cabin. He looked at Shukla, and shook his hand.

"How is your father Shukla? Did you speak to him? I hope all is well at home?"

"It's all because of your blessings, sir. I spoke to him this morning, and he has recovered a lot," Shukla replied.

"Come, Shukla! I need to talk to you about something important."

Shukla was anxious. He had known Ranjit for so long, but Ranjit had never spoken to him like this before. He went inside and Ranjit asked him to sit on the sofa. He told Shukla that there was some cash that needed to be delivered outside the state. Ranjit wanted to expand his business out of Mussoorie. To support this expansion, few contacts needed the money in hard cash, so he wanted the most trusted one for this job.

Shukla's first assignment was to collect a bag in two days, which contained fifty lakh rupees.

"I want you to drive the car, carry the bag and bring it back to Mussoorie. There will be more trips, so I want you to stay in Mussoorie for a while."

"I can do it, sir. But do you think my going alone will be safe?"

"I have asked my security to be with you. So, don't worry! But remember, they will go with you just for your safety. They won't know that the bag contains the cash." Ranjeet took a pause and said, "Listen, Shukla, this is the first time I am doing this. I can't trust any of them. You are my dependable support."

Finally, Ranjit convinced Shukla to take up this task.

•

Brajesh was planning to expand his empire from timber merchants to other business areas in the same city. But at the back of his mind, he was committed to toppling the dominance of Ranjit in the region. Deep down, he was sure that Ranjit had killed his father.

He was in desperate need to open a parallel investigation of his father's death. So, he called one of his old friends to Mussoorie.

Around 8 p.m., the doorbell rang. He opened the door and was delighted to see Vijay standing at the door. Vijay Pandit was Brajesh's school-mate. Brajesh was well connected with his school friends, and Jagan also knew a few of them.

"Welcome, Pandit! Welcome to Mussoorie. I hope you didn't have any difficulty in finding my house." Brajesh welcomed Vijay Pandit into his house.

"Who doesn't know Jagan uncle's house. You are the Alice of Timberland!" Pandit laughed.

"Pandit, I called you here to investigate into my father's death. Everyone in Mussoorie thinks that it was an accident, but I think it was a well-planned murder. It is not an allegation driven by emotions. I have solid points to prove this."

Brajesh sat on the chair near the firebox and lit up the fire. He could see that Pandit was feeling cold even inside the house. Once Pandit had become more comfortable, he continued, "Papa never used to drive the car. He felt that he was too old to drive on Mussoorie's curvy roads. We had a driver who used to take papa around and sometimes, even outside the city. He had just joined because before him, we had our most loyal driver, who died.

"One day, we heard the news that the driver fell from the hills and some man-eater tiger killed him. You know, a man-eating tigers are so rare nowadays. That too, in this part of the country! I was also shocked to hear that news. I was at Yale at that time. But when I saw the picture of his body and clothes, I was appalled. That kind of scars could only be done by a maniac or a psycho. I had no choice but to believe in the story.

"Later, when I came back from Yale, there was a rumour that the doctor had found iron chips inside his skin during the postmortem. They explained that someone, who was wearing an artificial iron-clad tiger claw, had torn his skin apart. Why would someone do that!

"Anyway, after his death, we got a new driver. One day when he was driving papa from the nearby forest, papa was hit by a truck and the car fell off the road. You would be surprised to know there was no trace of the driver anywhere.

"When the police found the car, papa's body was in the driver's seat. It was believed that my father was driving the car. The truck driver ran away, and he too, was never found. The only thing the police found was the dead body of my father and the crushed car. Nothing else. The planning was so accurate that not even a single evidence was found. No fingerprints, nothing!"

Brajesh became very depressed as he was narrating the story. Pandit came near Brajesh and tried to console him. He knew what Jagan meant the world to Brajesh. Brajesh was raised by a single dad and his father was his hero. When Jagan came to Mussoorie, he had nothing in his pocket. He started from scratch and made a mark for himself. During the journey, he had seen a lot of ups and downs in his life. Amidst poverty and loneliness, Jagan worked hard to build a successful empire, giving a great future to his son. Brajesh worshipped his father so much that he had kept his picture in the prayer room, above all gods.

Pandit went on his knees, kept a hand on Brajesh's shoulder, and said, "I am sorry, Brajesh. I know how much uncle meant to you."

Brajesh looked at Pandit. His eyes were wet, capturing the unimaginable pain of losing his father.

"Pandit, I want you to investigate the case. The local police are doing their job, but I don't trust anyone in the city now. Can you please dig out the truth for me?"

"I will," Pandit said with a smile.

Brajesh was elated to hear that. He told Pandit to not discuss the case with anyone. Pandit promised him that he would do everything possible in his capacity to find the truth.

Brajesh told Pandit that he would make arrangements for him to stay in a hotel. Pandit decided that he would only contact Brajesh over the phone now.

•

Pandit managed to find a house with one room and kitchen that looked like a studio apartment. He looked at various houses as he rode through the bustling lanes on his scooter. It had one balcony which opened towards the hill view of Mussoorie. He bought one sim card with a fake identity. Later, he went to more shops to purchase other essential items. While paying, he dropped a ten-rupee note on the ground.

"Sir, you dropped your money. Please keep it," a young boy said as he came running towards Pandit.

Pandit took that note and kept it in the pocket. As he was about to walk, he was again interrupted by the boy.

"Someone told me that when you drop the money on the floor, you should touch it on the forehead, pray to god, say sorry and then, keep in the pocket."

"Why to touch it on our forehead and say sorry?" Pandit asked him curiously.

"Because Lakshmi is the goddess of money and she won't be happy if you don't pray to her," the boy said.

Pandit chuckled. "Ah! Good to know that. Thanks for returning the money. Should I drop you somewhere? I can give you a ride," Pandit asked.

"Sure, I stay nearby," the boy said.

Pandit, while driving the scooter, asked him, "Do you work here or are you a student? And what's your name?"

"I work here, in the canteen in MJK college. My name is Arvind Ingle," I replied.

6

The Investigation Begins

I looked at Trivedi when that girl asked me for help. He signalled to me carry on, so I went to her table and sat down.

"See Aru, for the fest, the college management has asked me to escort an important guest around Mussoorie, but I won't be able to do it due to some urgent work. Can you fill in for me?" the girl said.

"I need to ask Trivedi first. But, why me?" I asked.

"Now, don't be so naïve. You know why I am asking you for help?"

"No, I don't," I emphasised.

"Aru, come on! I am talking to one of the most handsome guys in the college. Now listen, I want you to take him around the day when I would not be in Mussoorie," she said anxiously.

"But I haven't seen Mussoorie myself. How can I take him around?"

"I know that is a problem, but I have a solution for that. What are you doing this Saturday?"

"I will be studying for my exams," I replied.

"Take a break from study for one day. I will take you around Mussoorie. I will show you some spots where you can take Andre Bose," she replied.

"Andre Bose?"

"He is the speaker who is coming to our college for Yuva Utsav. Now listen, be ready on Saturday. Give me your phone number. I will call you before coming to pick you from your house."

"I don't have a phone."

"Okay, does Trivedi have a number?"

"Yes," I said and gave Trivedi's number to her.

When I went back to the counter, I told Trivedi everything. He was also surprised by her request. I asked if I could help her.

"I am fine with it, Aru, as long as you are not using your work time. Do you know her name now?"

"No, I don't," I replied .

"You don't even know her name and she is taking you for a ride around Mussoorie. You are going to get the biggest lesson of your life, my son," he chuckled.

•

That evening, when I almost reached my house after locking the canteen, someone honked from behind. I turned around and saw Pandit on the scooter.

"Hello, Aru!"

"Hi sir, how are you? What are you doing here?" I asked.

"Don't call me sir. My name is Pandit. Actually, I was looking for a truck driver. Do you know anyone who can help me?"

"No, I don't know anyone."

"Okay, anyway, would you like to come for a ride? Come, we will have some food together." Pandit asked politely. I was hungry so I couldn't say reject his offer.

We went to a street food shop on the mall road and stopped at one of the famous shops to eat noodles.

"What do you do for a living, Pandit? Did you come here for work?" I asked.

"No, not for work. I am roaming around to see Mussoorie and nearby places. This is one of the most beautiful places in India. They also call it 'The Queen of the Hills'. What an apt name!" Pandit said.

"So, what do you do in Mumbai?" I asked curiously.

"You want to know a lot of things, right?" He smiled and continued, "I am a freelancer. I worked in an IT company before, and now I have my own business." I was curious to know what or who a freelancer was.

Pandit explained to me that a freelancer is a self-employed individual who manages his work himself. There are also many websites for freelancers where one applies to get a job. A person has to quote an amount by bidding, and if clients want the job to be done at the money that is quoted, the client pays after the work is completed.

"What do you have to learn to be a freelancer? Do you need any college degree? Can a person like me do a freelancing job? How much can anyone earn there?"

Pandit said, "Aru, it looks like you have a lot of questions. Let me tell you all this while I drop you back home." So Pandit took out his scooter, and I hopped on.

"I build apps for mobile phones. You can do a good online course to learn the skill. You don't need any college degree to complete that course. Anyone can do it as long as you are keen to learn. In terms of earning, it depends on how many projects you can get for yourself. Sometimes, the earnings can go even in lakhs if you are able to bag high-paying projects. "

"Are you serious? I hope you are not kidding with me!"

"Yes, Aru, you can earn that amount. If you do well, you can also build your own company. " Pandit stopped the scooter near my house.

"What do I have to learn? Can you tell me more?"

"There are many courses. Nowadays, it is called Machine learning and Artificial Intelligence, A.I.," Pandit said thoughtfully. He could sense the excitement on my face.

"These are quite exciting words. I have never heard them before. I want to know more," I told Pandit.

"You can know more about them on the internet. Do you have a mobile?" Pandit asked.

"No, I don't have one."

"See, internet is the most important thing nowadays, Aru. It is a powerful way to get information. Don't deprive yourself of that knowledge. Buy a phone and keep learning," Pandit said.

"But, can I…?" I wanted to ask more about freelancers, but Pandit seemed to be in a hurry.

Hastily, I asked, "Can you give me your number?"

"Yes, but how will you call me?" Pandit asked.

"I will ask Trivedi to give me his phone," I replied with a smile.

•

The next day, Shukla came to our house. He wanted to change into more comfortable clothes before he started off with his long drive. I was alone at home as Trivedi had left for college earlier that day.

As Shukla came in, I asked him, "How are you, Shukla? Where have you been? Is everything okay?"

He replied annoyingly, "You ask too many questions, Aru. Do I look worried? No, I am not."

"Where are you going?"

"What is your problem? Did something happen? I am going to Delhi and will be back in two days. Let Trivedi know about it," Shukla picked up his clothes and walked out in a hurry.

"Will you drive the car?" I asked curiously.

"Then who else will drive? Let me go, Aru. Don't bother me," Shukla replied.

I had never seen Shukla so anxious before. After he left the house, I went out to see where he was going. I saw a big car with two men sitting in the back seat. Shukla got in and drove the car away.

•

Pandit drove into the woods to reach the place where Jagan was last seen. He decided to speak to people around the village outside the forest to know more about the events which took place that day. There was a small shop which sold some snacks, tea and cigarettes. Pandit decided to go there to find out more. He sat on the rickety bench and asked for a cup of tea.

An older man, in his late seventies, was supervising the stall. He gave Pandit a cup of tea. Pandit took a sip and said, "Uncle, have you been here for a long time?"

"Yes, long enough to tell you something about everything. What are you looking for?" the old man replied.

"I am here to see the jungle. It's a nice long drive from Mussoorie." Pandit did not tell the old man that he was a tourist.

"Jagan came here to meet someone. I don't know who it was. Even if you ask local villagers here, no one will tell you whom he met."The old man went back to his shop and turned off the stove on which he was making tea.

Pandit was surprised to hear what the old man just said. But at the same time, he realised that he was not the only one who had come here to look for Jagan's story.

"Who else came here, asking for him?" This time Pandit didn't hide anything and came straight to the point.

"Local police. And sometimes, his son," the old man replied.

"His son! Who?" Pandit was surprised.

"Brajesh Thakur, he is another one of his kind. He keeps coming here and asking the same question to everyone. Who met Jagan here that day," the old man responded.

Pandit was baffled by that discovery. This case was getting trickier. First, he hadn't been able to get any information about the truck driver. And now, he had to find out why Brijesh was seen around the jungle. While he was thinking about this conundrum, two guys came to that small shop. They had well-built bodies and seemed to be bodyguards or cops. They asked for cigarettes, looking sideways at Pandit.

Pandit had a lean appearance. He was wearing a casual jacket and jeans. They looked at him for a few seconds and then went back. When they returned to the jeep parked close by, Pandit asked the old man, "Who were they?"

"Police. They always come here, look around the jungle and go back. They have been coming here for the last two years since Jagan died. God knows what is hidden inside the jungle."

Pandit was disappointed, puzzled and lost. He sat on the scooter and started the engine. The old man shouted, "Do not go inside the jungle at night. People are saying nowadays that the man-eater is roaming around."

"Did you hear them roar anytime?" Pandit shouted.

"No, I haven't, but people say he took a few cows and men from the nearby village last month."

Pandit chuckled and drove the scooter back to Mussoorie. He came back to his hotel and called Brajesh.

"Hello Brajesh, how are you? Reached safely?"

"Yeah, all good. Tell me; do you have anything to share?" Brajesh asked curiously.

"Nothing much! I went to the forest where uncle was last seen, just before the accident. Have you been to that place before?"

"Yes, I have been there, just once. But in the villages, no one knows anything. Even if they do know something, they will not share as they are afraid of Ranjit. That guy has full control."

"You are in timber merchant business, is there any chance you want the trees to be cut? Are there any specific trees that you or Jagan uncle was interested in? Please tell me everything. Was Jagan uncle a part of any illegal business of cutting trees?" Pandit asked in suspicion.

"No way, Pandit. Yes, Papa was a timber merchant, but he always wanted to protect the forest. In fact, he was working very closely with a few NGOs to protect biodiversity. We have always been very ethical in this timber business." Brajesh was confident in his answer.

"But how did you know that Ranjit had so much control over Mussoorie? Have you heard anyone saying that? Or do you have a solid proof?"

"You are new to this city, Pandit. Slowly, you will get to know who controls Mussoorie. I am sure that Ranjit has killed my father and one day I will prove it," Brajesh said in an assertive way.

"I got your point, Brajesh, but I have to look at the case objectively. Unless I find some convincing evidence, I cannot hold Ranjit guilty. I want to look into it more. Do you know where I can get all the files related to Jagan uncle's investigation? I might need a copy. Can you arrange that for me?"

"I know the police officer who is in-charge of this case. I will ask him to get the latest copies of the investigation files and the FIR which was lodged when the incident happened."

7
Going Around Mussorrie

It was Saturday. Trivedi received a message on his phone from the girl who was supposed to pick me around 11 a.m.

Upon seeing the message, he came to me and said, "Look, Aru! I don't know why that girl is asking you to help her, but I don't get a good feeling about this. See, if at any point you feel that she is asking you to do something which you don't want to do, then just say no. Remember, there is no harm in exercising your freedom of choice." Trivedi was playing the role of a typical guardian.

I was very confused about the entire situation. I was constantly thinking about why she chose *me*. I had very few friends and this was the first time I was going out with a girl.

Will I be able to talk to her? What will I talk to her about? Will I make her feel awkward?

I had no answers to any of these questions. And to increase the anxiety, there was a question that kept striking my mind.

What is her name? I was sure that today, I would get the answer of at least this question.

•

After I finished my breakfast, she came to pick me up. I went out to see her. There she was, standing in a yellow kurta and white pyjamas. Her hair, which was still wet, was swirling down her ear. Holding the helmet in one hand and the other hooked to one of the handles, she waved at me to come quickly. As I came to her, my heart rate increased. I was set for an adventurous day.

When I reached near the scooter, she said, "Hey, thanks for coming. Now, let me tell you some ground rules. I will show you around Mussoorie, where you can take Andre. So, remember them properly. And most importantly, it is not a date. So, don't get wrong ideas." She chuckled and continued, "Let's not talk about it in college. Okay?"

While she was speaking, I was mesmerized by the beauty of her face. I didn't understand a word. All the while, I couldn't hear anything except my heartbeat.

She said, "Did you understand, Aru?"

"Yes," I replied, coming out of my reverie.

•

First, she took me to the hotel where Andre Bose was supposed to stay. Once we reached there, she said, "Aru, this is the hotel. Please go and look at everything properly. Ask me all the questions now, because next time, you will have to come here alone."

I got down and went inside. I went in and looked around. I saw two people who were sitting behind the reception desk. They were neatly dressed and had a smile on their faces.

As soon as I turned back, I saw Pandit. He came to me and said, "Hello, Aru? What are you doing here?"

"Hey, I came here with my friend for some work," I said, hoping to make the situation less awkward.

"Friend? Does he stay in this hotel?"

"No, she is waiting outside. I just came to see this hotel. Next Saturday, I need to receive someone here. So, I came to look around. Do you stay here?"

"Yes, I stay here," Pandit said.

•

After seeing the hotel, we went to see the Mall Road. There were a lot of small shops and eateries on the street. She pointed out a few of the famous ones and mentioned their speciality. I made a conscious effort to remember as much as I could.

After a while, it was noon, and we started to feel hungry. So we went to a restaurant which specialized in Tibetan food.

"Aru, what would you like to have? Have you eaten dim sums before? They have the best ones in Mussoorie." She sat at the table and asked me, flipping the pages of the menu.

I sat in front of her, folding my hands. "No, I haven't eaten dim sums before. How much does it cost?"

"Aru, this is on me. I will order dim sum for you and some fried noodles," she replied. She asked one of the waiters to bring that for us.

"Hey, I want to tell you something. I would really like to split the bill. If I can't pay now, then I will pay it later."

"Why? Because your *Aai* said so?" she asked me with a smile.

"Yes, and I would never disappoint her," I replied.

"Okay, mama's boy! I will split the bill. I will pay for now, and see the rest later?" She chuckled and continued, "Now relax and eat."

We finished lunch at the restaurant and went to the next stop, which was Bhatta Falls. There was a ropeway which was going down the fall. She showed me where I could get the ropeway tickets from. I followed her and listened to her instructions, but I was often tempted to see how it looked near the fall.

"Do you want to see how it looks? We can drive there and walk, instead of taking the ropeway."

"If you don't mind, yes, I would like to see," I said submissively.

"Okay, let's go then."

On the way down to Bhatta Falls, the stones were so granular that I could see her having difficulty walking down. Finally, we reached a point where there were chairs and a table kept in the water to dine. It was unique. While showing their surroundings, she slipped and I held her hand in split seconds. That was the first time I touched her hand. It was blissful.

I followed her and reached the next bigger waterfall ahead. The gust of water droplets was splashing our faces. Our hair was getting misty and our clothes were getting slightly wet. She was looking at the waterfall as if she was seeing it for the first time.

While walking back, I asked, "Have you come here before? I mean, you must have been coming here since your childhood?"

"Yes, of course, I have been here. But after my mother and father got separated, I didn't feel like coming here. This fall did not seem beautiful as it used to be when I came here with my parents," she said calmly and I was surprised to hear her story.

Then she turned back and said, "But today, after a long time, I don't know why, but it seemed really beautiful again," she chuckled and continued walking.

The story of her parents was bothering me. A child can't be split into two halves. How difficult it would have been for her when she came to know that she couldn't see her parents together, even though they were alive! I attempted to speak with her on this topic, but she was driving the scooter really fast. It wasn't easy to talk with the helmet on. So, I was quiet on the journey till we reached Kempty Falls in about forty minutes.

As she stopped the scooter, I got down and stood beside her. I was shivering due to cold.

"Aru? What happened? Are you okay? It looks like the jacket is not enough!" She quickly opened the boot of the scooter, pulled out a jacket and covered me with it. I could smell the sweet scent of the jacket. The fragrance was mesmerising.

She chuckled. "Well, that's a ladies' jacket, but it's fine. It looks more like unisex. Come, let's go! We have to walk. If you come with Andre, just ask him to buy tickets for the trolley if you don't want to walk. It is one of the most popular places in Mussoorie. So, he will ask you to come here."

I nodded and followed her to the Kempty Falls. It had a small pond where people could see inside, standing below the waterfall.

We briefly stood there and absorbed the magical view. While coming back, I asked her, "Do you miss your parents?"

She kept walking. I thought she had either ignored my question or didn't hear it. When we reached the scooter, she said, "Everyone is not lucky, Aru. Missing them is still bearable, but what's worse is that they are not together anymore. Anyway, we are done for today."

"I am sorry if I hurt you any way. I shouldn't have asked you about your parents," I said.

She came close to me. Then, she held my hand and said, "I am not hurt, Aru. So, don't' worry. In fact, I am staying with my grandmother. She is really nice and loving. Come, let's go."

It was evening and about to get dark. When she stopped the scooter next, I got down and started to walk towards my house. She was standing there and looking at me. After a few seconds, she shouted, "Aru!"

I turned back and looked at her. She waved me to come back. I briskly walked towards her.

"Thank you, Aru. It meant a lot to me." She again held my hand and continued, "After my parents got separated, I could not find anyone who was so understanding and comforting. You have something which belongs to me."

I was nervous. I could hear my heart beating loudly. I stammered and said, “What?”

“The jacket, you idiot!”

I was about to give it to her when she said, “You can keep it. It can remind you of the wonderful day we spent together. Thanks for your friendship again, Aru. It is precious!”

8
The Bag

Shukla was driving the car to Delhi. It was the first time that he was doing a job which involved a lot of cash, so he was extremely nervous. Once he arrived at Delhi, he reached the busiest area, which was close to Jama Masjid. There, he had to meet a wholesale shop owner named Jay Chandra. After reaching the shop, Shukla went inside alone. As per Ranjit's instruction, the guards were told to stay outside.

While Shukla was walking inside the shop, he saw there were piles of cartons placed alongside. And at the end of it, there was a small cabin where Jay was standing. He pointed Shukla towards a brown bag and said, "Don't lift it. Stroll it to the jeep. The handle will break if you try to lift it." His voice was heavy and authoritative.

When Shukla saw the bag, he started to sweat. His legs were shaking. Chandra said, "What happened? You can carry that, right?"

Shukla nodded his head and then, went to the suitcase. He pulled the handle, which could be extended, and tried to roll the suitcase. It was cumbersome. But, he managed to pull it out of the shop and went to the back of the SUV. Ranjit has asked to bring this bag back to Mussoorie.

As he sat on the driving seat, one of the bodyguards asked, "Shukla, you are sure this was the only work we had to do in Delhi. What's in the bag?" one of the bodyguards asked Shukla.

"Yeah, this is the *only* job we had to do. Sometimes I don't understand Ranjit sir, what is going on in his mind?"

Shukla was nervous that these guys didn't know about what was in the bag. What would happen if they came to know what was inside! He thought they could even kill him and take the money with them.

When he stopped the car briefly and went out, one of the guards checked the bag. He was astonished to find a lot of cash in it.

"There is money in the bag. Let's pick it up," the guard said excitedly. As they were about to carry the bag and steal the cash, Shukla smashed their heads with a thick stick. They started to scream and in a jiffy, Shukla jumped on to the SUV and drove it away.

The bodyguards were bleeding profusely. However, one of them was able to make a call. He said, "Hello, we are on the highway, around a hundred kilometres away from Mussoorie. Shukla is driving the SUV to Mussoorie. The bag is in the car."

The voice on the other side said, "How did you let him go! Idiots! Stay there! I will send someone to pick you up."

•

Shukla drove to Ranjit's house. He reached the gate and started to honk furiously, so that the security guard could open the doors quickly. Ranjit came outside after he heard the honking. The security guard opened the door and Shukla drove the SUV inside the house at great speed. Shukla narrated the entire story to him.

Ranjit was fuming after he heard what had happened. He dialled a number and shouted, "Someone tried to get away with the money. Who was behind it? Don't go to bed before you find out the truth."

Ranjit hung up. He hugged Shukla and said, "Now you know why I can't trust anyone. What you have done today can only be done by someone who is loyal to me. You are more than family, Shukla."

•

Around midnight, Ranjit's phone received a call. The caller told him the name of the person who was behind this incident.

Ranjit could not control his anger. He dialled a number and shouted, "I warned you before. Don't play these dirty games with me. I am giving you the last warning. Mend your ways!"

After a few seconds, a text message appeared on his phone.

It's not me! If I had to hit you, I would have done it from the front.

•

The next day, Shukla woke up at Ranjit's house. He requested Ranjit that he wanted to go home. Ranjit kept his hand on Shukla's shoulder and asked him, "Can you do this job again for me, Shukla?"

Shukla said, "Yes sir, I will do it. But this time, I don't need guards."

Ranjit looked at him. He smiled, and said, "Okay, this time I will let you do the job alone."

Shukla reached home and went to bed. While lying on the bed, he looked at me and said, "Aru, I am sorry. I was rude to you that day. I need to catch on some sleep, but please wake me up when Trivedi comes back."

I nodded and went back to studying. While reading, I flipped the pages and saw the pamphlet about the English-speaking course which I had brought with me a few days ago. I decided to find more details about the course.

After studying for an hour, I closed my book and walked to the institute office. The guy at the receptionist desk explained everything about the course, the job offer and the fees that I had to pay to get admission. It was a huge amount. I had to think more on this, so I decided to go back home.

Upon reaching home, I saw Trivedi and Shukla chatting with each other. Shukla mentioned a couple of times that he used to drive for Ranjit most of the time. Suddenly, I asked him, "Can you drive a truck also?"

Shukla stopped and chuckled, "Truck, no, I can't drive a truck. But, why do you ask?"

Trivedi said, "Oh, leave it Shukla! Someone met him here near our house who was looking for a truck driver."

I nodded and kept quiet.

9

The Bully

The next day, when I was in the canteen, the thought of joining a call center was swirling in my mind. After a while, I saw that girl walking inside the canteen. I thought of asking her about the course, so I went near her table and said, "Hi, can I ask you something?"

"Hey, how are you? Tell me how I can help you. Come, sit here," she said and smiled.

I told her all about the call center job and the course.

"Sounds good to me! But do you have that much of money to spend? See, anyone can appear for that interview. To learn English, you don't have to necessarily join the institute. You can learn by yourself as well," she said.

"But how can I learn on my own? Can you guide me?" I asked her curiously.

"You can learn it from educational videos and audio recordings. There are free tutorials available on the internet," she replied.

"But I don't have a phone to browse through the internet," I said in a disappointed tone.

"Okay, let me see you this evening. I will show you some free tutorials. See if that can help you."

She picked up all her books and walked out of the canteen. After she left, a few boys walked inside the canteen and sat on the table. They pointed at me and shouted, "Hey you! Come here."

I walked towards them. As I reached there, they said in a loud voice, "Tea for all of us, quick!"

I was annoyed by their behaviour, but I went inside and served them. They paid and I took the money. When I started to walk back towards the counter, one of them shouted, "Do you need a tip?"

I turned back and saw them waving at me. I went back to them again, and one of them got up from his place. He came close to me and yelled, "Listen, you moron! Here is your tip. A life-saving one. If we ever see you with that girl again, your charming face will be thrashed. Now, go!"

I stood there for a few seconds and went back to the counter.

After some time, that girl came to the counter and said, "I heard someone came here and bullied you. Is that right?"

I didn't say a word. She understood and said, "Don't worry, no one will bully you now. I will meet you later in the evening."

"If there is a problem, then you don't have to meet me. Really," I replied promptly.

"No, there is no problem at all. I will meet you today."

•

Around 5 p.m. she came into the canteen and asked me to come with her. She waited for me outside and when I reached, she started walking close to me. Sometimes our hands touched each other, which she didn't realize. But for me, those were thrilling moments.

After walking for a while, we sat on a bench inside the college campus. She hooked the left earphone in my ear and the right one in hers. She started to show videos and audio clips of people who were teaching how to speak in an American accent. She showed me many videos, but I couldn't concentrate on even one. While she was looking at the phone screen, I was gazing at her.

After a few minutes, when she was done showing the videos and audios, she said, "See how important it is to have a phone. Buy one for yourself, okay?"

I nodded my head.

It was late and Trivedi had already left for home. I was about to leave when she stopped me and said, "Come Aru, I will drop you."

When we reached home, she stopped the scooter and said, "Aru, I am sorry for what happened with you in college. The bullying and everything! You don't have to be scared at all. From today onwards, tell me whatever you want to share. I will listen to you and help you as much as I can."

"Thanks a lot," I said. Having a genuine friend in an unknown city was indeed a blessing!

10

The Mysterious Forest

Pandit went back to the forest to find some clues. He wandered around the houses near the forest and enquired about Jagan. But he couldn't find any information. He was tired and thought of coming back to that same shop. The old man was sitting on the chair and smoking a *beedi*.

When Pandit came towards him, he said, "There is something about this forest. Whoever comes here once, keeps coming here again and again!" Then, he paused and asked, "Do you want some tea?"

"Last time you told me that Jagan visited again and again. The truth is that he came only once," Pandit said and sat on the bench.

"Why would I tell you a lie? At this age, I have nothing to lose. It is up to you to believe me or not," the old man said. He switched on the stove and kept a dented aluminum bowl on it to make the tea.

"Did you know Brajesh? Have you seen him around many times? Why is no one telling me anything?" Pandit was frustrated.

The tea was ready after a few minutes. The old man poured tea and came to Pandit. "You have to find someone who has no fear of death. People here are scared. They will not tell you anything."

"Then, why don't you tell me what's there inside the forest? Why did Jagan come here? I knew Jagan was sincere and honest. He loved the forest."

"You are right. Jagan loved the forest. I saw him coming here with the NGO people sometimes. But, I have also seen him a few other times as well." The old man took a deep breath and continued, "Sometimes, greed for money can make you do anything. I know you have come here to find the truth. Why don't you go inside and find out?"

Pandit nodded and decided that he would go alone in the forest now.

"When you come back tomorrow morning, there is a Kali temple at a point where this village starts. People say that she takes care of everyone who goes inside the forest with pure intentions. Come early, pray there and tie a black thread around your neck. Kali *maa* will protect you from all evil."

•

The following day, Pandit came to the village. He stopped at the temple, bowed his head in front of Kali maa and asked the priest to give him the black thread.

The priest gave him the black thread and said, "If you are going inside the forest, keep your heart pure. Don't be greedy, or else this thread won't protect you."

Pandit nodded his head.

"Do you know what is inside the forest?" Pandit asked the priest.

"I only know that Shiva blesses this whole world. Jai Bhole Nath! He is the only one who knows everything." The priest smiled and went back inside the temple.

Pandit was walking down from the village to the foothill of the forest. The noise was slowly dying down. Due to misty weather, walking inside the forest was a difficult task. Pandit had come prepared, with trekking boots, a long walking stick, some food, and a rucksack filled with many water bottles. He started to follow a trail that was made by bicycles.

When he reached deep inside the forest, it was so quiet that he could hear his own breath. He kept looking around for some clues. The forest was filled with long oak and deodar trees. The mist was slowly getting dense and it wasn't easy to see anything beyond a few metres. The trail on which Pandit was walking suddenly disappeared. Now, Pandit had to walk on his own to ensure that he came back at the same point from where he started.

Having walked for almost two hours, he was tired. Pandit thought of taking some rest near a deodar tree. He took out the rucksack and kept it on the ground. He cleared the area so that he could sit and pulled out a couple of sandwiches from his rucksack. It was so tranquil that the warning calls of animals could be easily heard.

While eating sandwiches, he thought what he could do next. While he was in deep thought, he picked up some pebbles and started to throw them randomly. Suddenly, he heard as if the pebbles were dropping in water. He waited and looked in that direction. He picked up his rucksack and went in that direction to see what was in there.

A small lake appeared a few metres away. Surprisingly, the lake had no mist. It was in the shape of a crater and had flat land on the other side. On that land, Pandit could see a broken structure of the medieval temple, or perhaps a house on the tip of a vast green patch of land. He was amazed to see how a huge green patch of land in the forest suddenly appeared. It didn't look like a naturally built land. Nevertheless, it was a majestic view.

Pandit swiftly picked up his belongings, packed up everything and walked to reach the other side of the green patch. When he reached to the lake shore, he found that he could walk along the side of it. There was a small channel through where he could swim and reach on the green side. Pandit started to walk, but he had clearly underestimated the length of the periphery. It was long, but still he kept on walking.

After around an hour of walking, he reached the channel where he had planned to swim. It was tricky as it was really cold. Getting wet would have been nothing short of a nightmare. But,

Pandit has no other option. He took out the big plastic sheet and wrapped all his clothes, rucksack and everything else that could get wet. Then, he jumped in the lake with the plastic-wrapped rucksack.

Once he came out of the lake, he dried his body with his towel and quickly wore his clothes and jacket. He was still shivering. Then, he quickly collected dry leaves and burnt them using his pocket flint. Once the fire was lit, he started to feel warm.

Pandit decided that he would wake up after a quick nap. In a matter of seconds, he went into a deep sleep.

11

Learning English

When I reached home, Trivedi saw a radiant smile on my face. My eyes were sparkling with joy. When I reached my bed, he asked me again, "She dropped you, right? So my son, now do you know her name?"

"No, not yet. But one day I will. And that day will come soon," I chuckled.

"If you speak to your Aai today, let her also know about your new friend." He grinned.

I called up Aai that night. During the call, I told her about my ambition to learn fluent English for the call centre job. She reiterated that if I decide to learn fluent English, I should be firm on it and achieve the goal. She agreed to my decision of buying a phone and told me that she would send some money soon.

After finishing my call, I went to the box and deposited five one-rupee coins. The box had become much heavier now.

•

In college, that girl used to come every evening. We both used to listen to educational podcasts and watch online videos about how to speak in English.

One day, she asked, "You know Aru, how to spell a word on the call? I learned this yesterday. Let me tell you. Suppose you want to spell out a word to someone, for e.g. your name 'Arvind,' so how will you spell it?"

"How should I?" I asked curiously.

"It will be spelled like A for Alpha, R for Romeo, V for Victor, I for India, N for November, and D for Delta. This is how you will spell your name," she chuckled.

"That sounds great, let me practise it. Give me a name?" I smiled and asked, hoping that she would tell me her name.

She said, "Okay, let's take a simple name. How to spell the word Raj?"

I missed it. Now, I had no other option but to look for her name on the board.

"It should be R for Romeo, A for And…." I fumbled for the next word. "J for Juliet." I took a pause and asked her, "How was it? Correct?"

"A for Alpha Aru, not 'And'," She said and chuckled again.

By then, I knew that I was in love in her. Whenever I spent time with her, my brain stopped working and my heartbeats increased. But, did she also have feelings for me? I could only wonder!

"Aru, I think we are done with the introduction about fluent spoken English and self-learning video. Now that you are going to buy a new phone, you can continue on your own. I also have to prepare for Yuva Utsav. I will be around the campus, so if you need any help, come and find me. Okay!" she said.

"So, unless I find a new course to learn, we won't meet again?" I said.

"I will be there for you, in case you need any help," she said and smiled.

•

Later that evening, when I reached home, I saw Shukla and Trivedi discussing their childhood stories.

Shukla was talking about his driving experience where he was driving a truck. He said that he forgot that a truck didn't have a power steering. So, he dashed a milestone while driving a truck back in his village.

I turned to him and said, "But you had said, you don't know how to drive a truck."

"I? When did I say that?" Shukla replied surprised.

"Oh, that day, you remember someone came and asked Aru about the truck driver and he said there is no one here," Trivedi said and stood up to go to the washroom.

"Who was he Aru? Who was asking about the truck driver and why?" Shukla asked.

I didn't respond. I could observe that Shukla's facial expressions changed completely. He seemed to be angry.

I was baffled by what just happened.

12
The Manuscript

Pandit woke up after a long sleep. He saw the sun was over his head. He was having a severe headache and everything around him was spinning. He slowly picked up a long stick and looked around. He found himself near a temple. He saw that all the wood he had used to make bonfire was burned, but some of the dry leaves were half burnt. He picked up one leaf and tried to smell it. But, it did not have any fragrance. He looked around and saw a plant with the same leaf and flower bud. He plucked the flower bud and tried to smell it. The fragrance of the flower bud was exceptionally unique. It was like a stale aroma.

"Is it marijuana?" he said. He looked very closely everywhere to get more clarity. What he saw left him completely stunned. He was standing at the tip of a large field, filled with long grass and tons of hidden small marijuana plants. He has never seen such a massive field of this weed before. He discovered why he had a severe headache after burning those leaves because he was passively smoking marijuana the whole night.

But it also demystified the mystery of the jungle. It was weed. If exported, these weeds would be worth a million dollars.

He sat there, looking at the field and thought how much money one could make with this size of drug export. The words of the priest echoed through his mind.

Don't be greedy or else Kali maa will not protect you.

He had to get to the depth of this matter. He probed in further. He looked inside the rucksack. There were few sandwiches left and a pack of almonds. He ate all of it and drank some water. It was revitalizing and gave him the strength to continue his journey.

Taking that long stick in his hand, he walked inside the temple and the house adjacent to it. He opened the temple door. The sunlight was coming through the cracks in the roof. He went inside and saw a deity. It was god Shiva, almost six feet tall. There was dirt all over it. It looked like no one had visited that temple for ages. He went close to it and removed the dust with his handkerchief. Below the thick layer of dust, the surface was shining, and when sunlight fell on it, vibrant red hues could be seen. He discovered that the whole statue was made of ruby stone which was worth a million dollars. He had stumbled upon a hidden treasure.

Later he went inside the broken house. There were only a few items – a small metal trunk and clothes which were covered in dirt. He removed some items from the shelf while looking around.

Suddenly a bundle of palm-leaf manuscripts fell from the top. It was so fragile that some of it broke from the sides when it fell off. Pandit cautiously collected all of them and brought them out of the house. He took out his phone and clicked some pictures of the deity idol.

•

When Pandit went back to Mussoorie, he reached the hotel and took a cold shower. After the shower, he felt refreshed like never before. The first thing he did was to open the palm leaf to look at the manuscript. He couldn't understand anything so he took out his DSLR camera, zoomed the images of the palm leaf and started to take pictures of each of them.

One of his friends Milan Singh, was a historian and archaeologist. So, he dialled his number to seek his advice.

"Hello Milan! How are you, my brother?"

"Hi Pandit! I am good. How can I help you? Did you stumble upon something interesting?" he chuckled.

"Milan, I am sending you some images of manuscripts written on palm leaves. Help me to translate what is written on it," Pandit said.

"Wow, Pandit! What are you up to now? Anyway. I will get back to you on this.

After sending the pictures to Milan, Pandit browsed across all the messages he had received in the meantime. He got one message from Brajesh where he had mentioned about Vishal Dubey and his phone number. He would be the one to provide the FIR copy of Jagan's case and some other investigation report as well.

He called Vishal, who agreed to meet him in a café to help him.

•

"Vishal, does this document have all the information about Jagan's accident and preliminary investigation?" Pandit asked.

"This is all that I have and probably, what you need. The teams are working on it to investigate more, but there is hardly any evidence here. The document has the details of what the police saw at the accident site. People's statements and pictures are also in the document. But we were not able to find the truck driver and Jagan's driver. They disappeared without a trace. Although, we do know that the truck was coming from Delhi."

"Who is the truck owner?" Pandit asked curiously.

"The owner is from Delhi, a wholesaler of spare parts. Someone known as Jay Chandra. He had filed an FIR about the truck being stolen a week before the accident happened. We investigated him, but he was clean. Apparently, the truck was never seen in Delhi after he reported. The only time it was seen was on the accident day," Vishal replied.

"Is there any connection with Ranjit here?" Pandit asked.

"Jay Chandra was seen with Ranjit in Mussoorie, in an event. So, suspicion is on him, but if Jay is clean, we cannot say anything. And Ranjit is a big name here. Jagan was a small trader. What benefit did Ranjit get by getting Jagan killed?"

"So, you think Ranjit is not behind this?" Pandit asked.

"It hardly matters what I think. The case is still open and everyone is on the radar. You can have a look at the document and decide for yourself. But I do have a suggestion. Stay away from the police investigation. There are supporters for both Ranjit and Brajesh, who are closely involved in the investigation. I know you are close to Brajesh, but he can do anything to get Ranjit behind bars on this case."

13

Andre Bose

The day had come when I had to go and pick up Andre Bose from the hotel to show him around Mussoorie. I wore a wrinkle-free shirt, smart trousers and flip-flops and went to the hotel where Bose was staying. I went inside and reached the reception desk, asking for Bose. He was sitting and having his tea. Someone ushered me to him. I introduced myself as a student from MJK College.

He scanned me. Surprisingly, he said, "I was expecting someone else to be here to greet me."

I asked promptly, "Yeah, that girl? She can't come because of some urgent work at home. However, I am at your service. I will guide you and show a few good places across Mussoorie."

He frowned and gave me a strange look.

"You study in MJK?" I nodded my head. And with disappointment, he stood up and said, "How can the management send someone like you, who just walked into a hotel, wearing flip-flops?"

His car arrived and he invited me to join him. I opened the door and sat in the front seat, even before Bose sat in the car. This time Bose got really annoyed, seeing that I hadn't opened the door for him, or waited for him to sit inside, as was common courtesy.

While we were still on the Mall Road, Bose asked me, "What is your subject in engineering?"

I am in the second year..." I stammered.

"Yes, but which subject? I mean computers or electronics, what is your major in?"

"Electronics," I fumbled.

I could sense that he was not impressed with my answer at all. Even though he was a motivational speaker, his presence was deeply unsettling.

Gradually, he figured out that I was not a student, but trying to impersonate one. He was so annoyed that once we got out of the car, he asked me in a loud voice, "What do you do, Arvind? I don't think you are even from MJK!"

I said in a shaky voice, "I am a canteen boy."

He said arrogantly, "MJK has sent a canteen boy to receive me! This is how they welcome a personality like me," he said angrily and went to his room.

I never expected such a response from a highly influential motivational speaker. That day I realized how the world perceived me. I was not valued for my goodness. Rather, my worth was determined by the kind of clothes I wore.

I felt very disappointed, but my decision to join the call center became firm now.

•

The next day, when I was working in the canteen, that girl stepped in excitedly and asked, "How was it? Did you show him Mussoorie? Was he happy?" She smiled and asked.

"Where were you? Why didn't you pick him up? Why did you choose me?" I said in an annoying voice.

"Yesterday was the most beautiful day, Aru. Thanks for backing me up." She was blushing, which made her look even more beautiful. I looked at her and my frustration vanished.

"Yes, you were saying something?" she asked me. I was about to tell her the truth, but she seemed so happy.

I said, "Nothing, it was okay. He liked Mussoorie a lot."

"Obviously, he will like it. After all, he was with such a handsome boy. You must have impressed him," she chuckled and continued.

"Listen, tomorrow, he has a session after 2 p.m. I want you to be there. I will book the seat for you in the front row. Don't miss that session. Promise me that you will be there." She extended her hand towards me.

I kept my hand on it and said, "Yes, I will be there."

•

MJK also had a blood donation camp going on. I told Trivedi that I would also like to donate blood. He was happy and asked me to go for it. Although, it was a long queue, I was happy to see the turnout for such a good cause. When my turn came, the doctor asked me about my blood group. I didn't know, so she said that she will test the blood group first and then will take the blood.

The blood test came out quickly. She was surprised to tell me that my blood group is AB negative, which turned out to be the rarest in the world.

14
New Clue

Ranjit called Shukla to talk about the next trip. After the first trip, he was feeling more confident. Looking at him, Ranjit knew that he had discovered one of the best men for the job.

"Shukla, I am happy to see you back. This time you have to take a suitcase from me and exchange it for another one. It means that you will have to be very cautious. Can you do it?" Ranjit asked Shukla.

"What is inside the bag, sir? If I may ask?" Shukla asked Ranjit.

"Don't worry about what is inside the bag. Just know that it is very precious to me."

When will I have to take the bag for the delivery?" Shukla asked curiously.

"Tomorrow night you will start from here. And come back the day after tomorrow," Ranjit replied.

•

Pandit was looking at the documents which Vishal gave him. He read through the FIR report and all the eyewitnesses' statements when the accident happened. The next thing he wanted to see was the accident site. He also wanted to meet the two eyewitnesses – One was an eight-year-old boy and another was a fruit seller.

Pandit went to the fruit seller's house first – Ram Kumar. When he reached his house, he was not there. Pandit got to know that Ram Kumar had gone to the city for a job. But the police had asked him to come every month and report at the local police station. So Pandit thought that he would come back later to speak to him, probably at the end of the month. Then, he rode his scooter to the village where the small boy lived. He was his last hope.

Pandit reached the house, asking people. It was a small hut where two kids were playing in the mud outside. This boy was weaving a broken chair with the plastic rope, which had multiple knots on it. It looked like he had collected all this from the roadside or the garbage lying around.

Pandit went to him and asked about what he had seen that day. To which he replied, "I have told everything to the police. There is nothing I know more than that. I have asked them to give me some money. I have to feed many younger brothers, but they kicked me out. Those are very bad people. I will not tell them anything. You are also the same. Go away!" The boy said and started crying.

Pandit opened the boot and brought some bread, snacks, juice and water bottles. He collected all of that and went straight inside the hut. The boy followed him inside.

He kept everything on the bed and said, "Please eat whatever you want. I will talk to you later."

Both his younger brothers came running inside. They were thrilled to see a lot of food on the bed. They jumped with joy and started to open the packets. This boy was smiling, looking at Pandit. He pulled Pandit out of the house and told him what he had seen that day. He went in and brought a dirty glove made with wool with him and gave it to Pandit.

"When I saw the driver running away after hitting that car, these gloves fell off from the truck's driving seat."

"Then why didn't you give these to the police?" Pandit asked.

"They didn't give me food when I asked for it, why should I give it to them?" The boy replied.

Pandit took out a five-hundred rupees note from his pocket and gave it to the boy. He now had a critical piece of evidence.

It had been almost two days, and there was nothing from Milan about the manuscript on the palm leaf. He was getting restless now.

15

Shortcut to the Top

After receiving the money order from Aai, I decided to buy a phone for myself. I went to a few mobile shops located on the Mall road. While walking, I saw Pandit at one of the grocery stores. I told him that I was buying a phone which made him really happy. After he finished his grocery shopping, he came out with me and said, "Why do you want to work in a call center? The technology is advancing at a rapid pace. Learn computer programming. It's the most demanding field. I told you earlier about my experience as a freelancer, you remember?" Pandit asked.

"Yes, I remember. But I am not sure if I would be able to write those complex codes. I don't know anything about that field. At least I know a little bit of English. I can improve on it and get a decent job for myself," I said.

"See, if you have not tried learning about a computer, then how can you say that you cannot do it? It's like giving up before trying," Pandit said while opening the boot of the scooter. When the boot opened, I saw a dirty piece of gloves in it. I was wondering why he was carrying such a muddy glove.

"Do you use that glove to wipe the scooter?" I asked him surprisingly.

Pandit laughed, "No, it's an important thing. I can't use it for wiping the scooter." Then we walked towards the shops to buy the phone, leaving the scooter behind.

After a long hunt, I finally got a phone which fulfilled all my basic requirements. Pandit insisted that he would drop me home. While we were coming back on the scooter, I asked him.

"Did you find any truck driver for your work?"

He replied, "Oh, I remember. But I don't have a truck. It was just a casual inquiry. Why are you asking? Do you know anyone?" Pandit chuckled.

"Yes, I know one," I replied.

Pandit stopped the scooter and parked at the side, it was just before my house. He asked me:

"Who is he?"

"He is not a regular truck driver, but he drove a few times. Currently, he is working with someone already, so I don't think he needs any work at the moment," I said.

"It's fine. But who is he? Can I meet him?" Pandit was curious to know.

"Yes, you can meet him. He is my roommate, Shukla. But he is often away for work purposes. There is a businessman here named Ranjit Singhania. He is quite a big name in Mussoorie. Shukla is lucky to work for him," I said.

"See Aru, I am not sure when he will come back. But can you do me a favour?" Pandit asked.

"Yes. Tell me!"

"See here..." he opened the scooter boot and took out the gloves. He asked me to take out my phone so that he could take a picture.

Pandit said, "See these gloves, now I will take picture of it from your phone. When you meet Shukla next time, just ask him if these gloves belong to him? Whatever is his response, just message me. Okay?"

I was surprised by his strange request. I nodded, hoping that it had some relevant purpose.

•

It was the last day of Yuva Utsav. Everyone was excited to attend the Andre Bose session which was supposed to happen in the afternoon. I wanted to learn from him, so I wrapped up my work at the canteen and went to find the auditorium.

When I reached, I saw that girl. She took me inside the auditorium from the back door. I tried to say something, but she turned and said, "Aru, quickly go in now. Look for seat number A11. I have reserved it you."

I followed her instructions and sat on my seat. I was sitting very close to the stage, which made me slightly nervous. Andre Bose could have easily spotted me.

After a few minutes, all the lights in the auditorium were dimmed. The curtain was opened and Andre Bose walked in. Everyone gave a standing ovation. After a few minutes, he asked them to sit down. He took the mic out from the stand and started walking around the stage.

"You are young India. Look at you! Energetic, intelligent, charismatic, and ready to conquer the world. Keep your spirits high when you leave the campus after graduating from MJK. Great companies are waiting for you. Join them to solve the problems they can't even see right now. But remember one thing; don't lose hope. Have you seen a lion? Is he bigger than an elephant?" he asked everyone.

"No," everyone replied in unison.

"Is he bigger than a giraffe?"

"No!"

"Is he bigger than a bison?"

"No," the crowd said. This time, I joined them too.

"But when the lion runs towards them, they all run for their lives. Do you know why? Because when a lion looks at them, he thinks of them as his prey. The lion is fearless. This is why a lion is the king of the jungle. Be fearless like a lion. Always roar in your life."

The entire crowed started to clap. I was so inspired by what he said that it gave me an electrifying feeling.

He took a pause and looked around again. "Now, I will tell you a bitter truth. Until you achieve what others consider to be impossible, no one will believe you. Nobody will applaud for until you show impressive results. You must never forget, that work comes before belief. You have to work hard when nobody is there to pat your back. Remember, a great life is in front of you, not behind you."

Listing to Andre Bose was mesmerizing. I felt that I could achieve so much in my life. Andre Bose continued, "I would also like to say that you should never be embarrassed by the truth of your life. Try to embrace it and focus on learning." When I started to clap loudly, Andre Bose recognized me.

His expression became intense. Maybe because he was not expecting to see a canteen boy sitting in the front row.

He continued, "Now listen to this very carefully. Sometimes you have to look for people in your life from whom you want to stay away. There are people who want to avoid all the hard work and struggle. They take shortcuts to reach to the top. Let me show you an example." He paused and looked at me.

"Hey you, there! Come up..." He pointed his hand towards me.

I got nervous and slowly walked up the stage. When I reached, Andre Bose pulled me towards him and said, "You know who he is? He is a canteen boy, in your college. Imagine, someone like him, sitting in front while deserving students like you are sitting at the back. Look at him! These are the people you should look out for. They will find a shortcut to reach the top, always."

I felt really ashamed, standing in front of the entire college. I looked at that girl. She was shocked. Tears were flowing endlessly from my eyes. That day, I hated myself.

He kept talking, "This boy even came to me to show me Mussoorie. Imagine! How many of you know which hotel I am staying in? I will not ask him how he did it. But would rather emphasise the point I am making. Just remember, never to take shortcuts in life."

I was standing there, with my head down.

When he finished his speech, I came down the stage. I looked for that girl, but she was not there. Andre Bose kept talking more, but I could not process anything. I was numb. I could not bear to stay there any longer and rushed out.

16
The Confession

"Aru, stop!"

Her voice stopped me as I was going towards the canteen.

"I am sorry for whatever happened inside. I didn't know that Andre would treat you like this. Please forget about it. Look at life differently. The reason I was not able to receive Andre was because I had to be with my boyfriend for his birthday celebration. You can't imagine how happy he was when I reached his house. I asked him to come to college today, so that I could introduce you to him.

I kept listening to her and tears started to roll down my eyes.

"Don't cry Aru, please. I am really sorry."

I kept my hand on her shoulders and said, "You know something? I don't even know your name. And yet, I kept listening to you and fulfilled your requests. Do you know why? Because I have feelings for you."

"Aru, what are you saying? I have always looked at you as a good friend. I mean, you are a canteen boy. How is it even possible?"

"You are right! I am just a *canteen boy*. It was my mistake to even consider a possibility with you. But, I was living in my own bubble and Andre just brought me back to reality."

While we were talking, someone came from behind and said, "What happened?You guys okay?" He tapped on her shoulder and frowned.

She nodded her head and said to him, "I wanted you to meet him. Rahul, he is Aru. He is a…"

I stopped her in between and said, "A canteen boy. I sell tea in MJK."

"Aru, he is Rahul Singhania."

I smiled and shook his hand.

"How are you, Rahul? You are lucky to get a girl like her. I don't know if I can even say this because I am just a canteen boy. Anyway, I should get going now."

I started to walk away, but she came behind me.

"Aru, wait!"

I turned around and told her, "Can I ask you for one help? I don't want to be a *canteen boy* for my entire life. I want to work hard, study and build my future. Please forgive me if I don't meet you in the canteen from now on. Life has taught me a lot today. It's good for me to start afresh and push the reset button in my life."

I walked out from there and went to the canteen. Trivedi asked me how it was.

"It couldn't have been better than this. My life has completely changed in the last two hours."

•

Shukla came into the house and started to pack the bag for his next trip. Meanwhile, we started to prepare for dinner. I thought it was a good time to show Shukla my new phone and ask him about the gloves.

In the kitchen, I showed Shukla my phone and he loved it. While showing the phone I went to the picture gallery and opened the image of the glove.

"Nowadays, it's very cold outside. My hands get frozen sometimes. I need to keep rubbing it to keep it warm."

Trivedi said, "It's nothing Aru. You may even see snowfall here."

"I am feeling cold already. I seriously need gloves to wear," I said.

"Then, buy from Mall Road. There are a lot of good shops there," Shukla said.

"Yeah, I saw one glove while I was walking around to buy my phone. Such beautiful gloves lying on the road, so I took a picture with my new phone," I said.

"Show me which one you are talking about?" Trivedi asked me. I opened the picture and showed it to him.

He looked at it and said, "Yeah, looks good! But it's so dirty. Where did you find it? And wait… wait… I have seen this before. I had a similar glove."

He took the phone and showed it to Shukla and said, "See Shukla, aren't these the same gloves you had? You had even lost one glove of the pair."

Shukla looked at the phone. He was surprised to see the gloves. He stammered, "Yeah! These are just like mine. I haven't found the other one even till now. I think I might have lost it somewhere."

I was shocked to know that the gloves belonged to Shukla. I thought of letting Pandit know about it. However, I still didn't know why he wanted me to check with Shukla on this. I didn't want to hide anything from Shukla, so I decided to tell him everything.

I would meet Pandit, but wouldn't tell him that Shukla knows everything.

I sent a message to Pandit.

Hi, I have something to tell you. Can we meet tomorrow?

After a few minutes, I got a response.

Let's meet tomorrow in the evening around your house.

17
Critical Case

The next day, Shukla went to Ranjit's home in the morning. When he reached the house, he saw an ambulance standing at the gate. Shukla was shocked to see it and rushed from the main gate inside the house. When he reached near the door, he saw Ranjit coming out with a doctor.

"What happened, sir? Why do we have an ambulance here?"

"There is a big problem, Shukla. Rahul is not well. He fainted in the morning. We called up the doctor who suspects that it could be kidney malfunctioning. We will have to find a kidney donor for him. The difficulty is that his blood group is very rare, AB negative. It's so difficult to find any donor with this blood group."

Shukla said, "Don't worry sir! God will help you through this. Have faith in him."

"Thanks, Shukla," Ranjit replied.

"Sir, I will carry on with the trip tonight. Don't worry about it. I will collect the bag from you before I leave for Delhi," Shukla replied and left. Ranjit went inside the house and sat near Rahul.

Rahul looked into Ranjit's eye and said, "Don't worry dad, I will be okay. See, I am smiling, isn't it?"

"Yes, my son, you will be fine. I will go to every corner of the world to find someone who can donate his kidney. Your dad is not that helpless." Ranjit said and smiled. He hugged Rahul tightly and said, "I love you Rahul! Don't worry, I will make everything right."

One servant came into the room and said, "Sorry to disturb you, sir. One madam has come to meet you."

Ranjit looked at Rahul and said, "Is she the lucky one?"

Rahul smiled and said, "Yes."

Ranjit smiled and walked out of the room.

•

Shukla returned home. I told Trivedi that I would be late for the canteen so I was at home. I noticed that Shukla looked upset again.

"Hey Shukla, worried about today's trip?" I said.

"No, I am not worried about it. You know Ranjit's son, he is critical. Ranjit was saying that there might be a kidney failure. He is looking for someone who can donate a kidney to his son. And the worst part is that Rahul's blood group is very rare. It is difficult to find a donor with that blood group," Shukla said and went into the kitchen to get some water.

"What is his blood group?" I asked.

"It's AB negative," Shukla replied and gulped the water.

"That's rare; I also came to know very late," I replied.

"How do you know about it?" Shukla asked.

"I know because I have the same blood group."

Shukla frowned and started to cook food for himself.

I thought of telling Shukla about about my meeting with Pandit. But I first wanted to know why Pandit was asking about those gloves.

•

That evening, before leaving for home, I texted Pandit that he could come. He was there even before I reached. Pandit was waiting for me eagerly, to know the answer. I saw him standing near the scooter and waved at him.

I said, "Pandit, I will tell you what Shukla said. But before that, you have to tell me the story behind this glove. Why are you so curious to know it?"

"Aru, this is not the right time to tell you everything. But I promise, when I know the truth, I will certainly tell you," Pandit replied.

"No Pandit, I need to know right now," I insisted.

"Please tell me how is Shukla related to this," I said and looked into his eyes.

"It means this glove belongs to Shukla. Is that right, Aru?" Pandit said in a commanding voice.

I was quiet and nodded my head. There was a silence between us.

"I want you to promise me that if Shukla is in trouble, then you will tell me first. You will help him."

"I can't promise that to you, Aru. I can just hope that you won't tell Shukla about it," Pandit said.

"Why are you here, Pandit? Why did you come to Mussoorie?" I asked.

"Listen Aru, I am here to find the truth regarding a case in which these gloves will play a pivotal role. Local police won't know about it. Now in this city, only you know what I am doing here. I can't tell you who I am working with, but I am helping one of my oldest friend," Pandit said.

"Is Shukla safe? Did he do anything wrong?" I asked him.

"I can't tell you that now, but if he is innocent, then nothing will happen to him. I promise you, Aru."

•

I reached home and was eagerly waiting for Shukla. When I saw him, my heartbeat increased. I didn't know where to start. While I was looking for him, he asked, "Aru, what happened?"

I took a deep breath and said, "Shukla, someone is looking for you."

"Again, for work? You know I am busy working with Ranjit," Shukla chuckled.

"It is not for work Shukla," I replied in a shaking voice.

"Not for work? Then for what?" Shukla looked at me.

I told him everything about Pandit's case.

"What is the connection between the truck driver, this glove and you? Tell me Shukla, did you do something wrong?"

Shukla's face turned pale. He asked, "Was he from the police?"

"No," I replied.

"Aru, I need your help. I want you to get all the information from him. I am like your family. You should help me, please," Shukla begged.

"But you have to tell me everything, Shukla? What is the matter?"

"I will tell you everything once I am back from Delhi. Please trust me," Shukla said and walked out of the house.

•

Shukla went to Ranjit's house to take the bag. It was a huge suitcase, so he rolled it into the car. He drove the car for three hours and found a spot that was quiet and dark. After parking the car, he tried to open it, but it was locked. Luckily, he found one small screwdriver and opened it from the side. He pushed through the small gap that was created, and suddenly, a small packet came out. It was covered with black plastic.

Shukla took a knife and tore the packet. He removed the first layer of plastic. After that layer, he saw a banana leaf tightly wrapped up on a solid object. He tried to remove the banana leaf and found a green paste, a semi-solid thing.

Curiously, he took out and tried to smell. It was a pungent smell; he knew he was smelling marijuana paste. Shukla was shocked to discover that he was shipping drugs out of Mussoorie, and Ranjit was asking him to do it without telling him. He was terrified that if the police stopped the car, he would be behind bars. But he couldn't do anything about the shipment now. He had to deliver it.

This time, he knew Jay Chandra's location.

•

In the morning around 10 a.m., Jay came. He went near the shop, pulled up the shutter and waved at Shukla to come in. Shukla went inside and left the suitcase inside the SUV. After a few seconds, a black Toyota car came and stopped outside the shop. Two people rushed inside, took out a pistol and shot Jay. They shot four bullets and ran away. Shukla was terrified to see this. He kept hiding behind the cartons till they left in the car.

Jay was soaked in blood. Shukla saw that two bullets had hit him in his chest and two on his head. His eyes were open, one hand was on the chair and the other one was on a brown suitcase. Shukla removed Jay's hand, pulled that bag handle out, rolled it out of the shops, and ran away from the site. He left behind the blood trail which were made by the wheels of the suitcase, drenched in Jay's blood.

Few people saw the shooters running away in the car. The shooters ran the car with the full throttle and went inside the adjacent lane. After a few metres, they hit the electric pole so hard that the live electric wires fell on the car. All of them got electrocuted. People rushed to save them, but it was too late. The car's petrol tank started to leak with the impact, and a small spark of the electric wires ignited the car. The fire spread so fast that within a minute, black fumes started to come out of it.

There was complete chaos in the lane. Unaware of this chaos, Shukla drove the SUV back to Mussoorie.

•

Finally, Pandit received a mail from Milan Singh. The one he was desperately waiting for. After the mail reached him, Milan called Pandit.

"Pandit, I understood what was written on the palm leaves. It is written in Odia script. It's about Shaivism. You know, this text is basically about Shiva. It talks about the Shiva avatars and his devotees. I am still trying to convert all the details into English, but overall, it mentions Shiva's presence in some field, saying he has cursed something. He is with a demon that has brought Shiva there. I can say only this much at the moment. It will take me more time to understand what the entire manuscript means. But, thought of letting you know how far I have reached."

"Thanks a lot, Milan. You are a genius. I will wait for you to translate it completely in English. But this is a good start."

"But it does not mention anything about crime. I am not sure you will get anything from it," Milan said.

"It is fine Milan. I will have to figure that out. Anyway, thanks, brother," Pandit chuckled.

Pandit was trying to connect what Milan said about the scripts on the palm leaves to what he saw in the field. He had a plan in his mind. He would not tell Brajesh about him finding out that the truck driver is Shukla. Because Shukla was employed by Ranjit.

Pandit was starting to believe that Ranjit was behind Jagan's killing.

•

Next day in the canteen, Trivedi said that Professor Mishra was busy in his lectures. So, he wanted tea to be served to him in his classroom. Professor Mishra was the computer programming professor. He was well respected among students.

I was honoured to serve him tea during his lectures. I took the tea and went into the classroom where he was conducting the lectures. On the board, it was written 'Artificial Intelligence'. The topic seemed familiar to me.

Prof Mishra had a projector set up in the classroom and all the students were with their laptops. I was amazed to see that kind of classroom setup.

After giving him tea, I decided to stand outside the room and listen to what he was saying about it.

"Do you know what artificial intelligence is? Anyone?" Professor Mishra asked.

"It's a wide range of computer programs and algorithms that is fed into the machine so that it mimics the action that is similar to human intelligence and capability," a student responded.

"Good. But let me explain in simpler terms. Artificial Intelligence, which is referred to as A.I. is the intelligence which machines demonstrate to us, like a human being. It may seem natural, but it is artificial. So, we call it 'Artificial intelligence or A.I'," Professor Mishra said.

Professor Mishra's lecture was so interesting and simple that I stood near the gate and kept listening to him.

He continued to talk about Artificial Intelligence (A.I.) and its history. His lecture lasted for one hour. That one hour ignited my curiosity to learn more about A.I.

Once the lecture was over, I went back to the canteen and started to browse videos on A.I. and machine learning. Most of the videos were for experts and no one could explain the way Professor Mishra was explaining to the class. So, I decided that I will speak to Pandit and understand from him.

18

Bitten by the AI Bug

I met Pandit near my house. I told him about Professor Mishra's lecture and how his lecture had inspired me to learn more about A.I.

"That's good Aru, that you want to learn more about A.I. I told you, unless you step foot into the water, you would never know how to swim. So, go for it. There are few online lectures about basic programming and machine learning. Listen to them and see if that is easy for you to understand. Else I will guide you wherever I can," Pandit replied.

That evening he showed me some online resources to study the basics of machine learning and programming.

"Aru, I hope you haven't told anything to Shukla about this," Pandit asked.

I silently nodded my head and stood quietly.

"See Aru, there are a lot of things that I need to uncover. I have got an answer to just one question and there are many more left. I am doing what is good for Shukla at this time. If he knows that I am looking for him in a case, he might take some steps that will not be good for him. I hope you understand what I mean."

"I understand, Pandit. I also hope that you will tell me what are you investigating and how deep Shukla is in trouble," I said to Pandit.

That night, I listened to all the lectures and understood the concept of programming and machine learning. I made copious notes. Finally, I filtered out the first few programming languages that I would learn.

But the next problem in front of me was to get a computer where I could run the code. Since it was not possible in the initial days, I decided that I will write the codes on paper, instead of running the codes on the computer.

I took out a notebook and created a bookmark by folding a paper in the middle of the notebook.

At the top of the first page, I wrote, *Python – Basic of Programming language*. Back then, I never thought these five words would change my life forever.

•

The next day onwards, I started following Prof Mishra's lectures. I noted down his lecture's timing and the names of the other teachers who taught programming languages to students. I found out that Prof Mishra was the only one who taught students basic and advanced programming. Python programming language was one of them. I tried to figure out how far had he reached in his lectures. The best way to do that was to keep my ears open and listen to the students who visited the canteen.

I spotted someone among the students who attended Prof Mishra's lectures. I took the table cleaning mop, went beside them, and started to mop slowly so that I could listen to what they were saying.

"Tomorrow, Prof Mishra will start basics of Python." One of the students spoke to his friends. Then, he saw me and whispered, "Hey, watch out for the shortcut!" All of them laughed loudly.

That day, I found out that I had got a new name after the Andre Bose incident, 'The Shortcut.' Life had just begun to throw challenges at me and I was geared up to take them, head on.

•

I went to Prof Mishra's lecture and stood outside. He started with the topic on the board "Python – Basic." The class was full and there was pin-drop silence.

The first chapter that he taught was similar to what I had learned online. So, some of the topics were easy for me to understand. I quietly switched on my mobile phone to record what he was saying. Those were my notes from the lecture.

Prof Mishra had an interesting way of keeping students engaged. There was a blackboard outside the class. Every month, Prof Mishra used to write one problem statement related to the programming language that he was teaching. Prof Mishra used to ask the class the next day if anyone had managed to solve the problem.

I decided to keep a track of the board to learn more.

19

The Eye Witness

Shukla returned from Delhi that evening. He stopped before Mussoorie to think what he should do next. He was sure that Ranjit might not have received the news about Jay.

There were two options in front of him – either he could give the bag to Ranjit and say that he would not do any more such trips. Or, he could keep both the bags with him and tell Ranjit that the shooters took away both the bags with marijuana. This way Ranjit would stop these trips till he got any new clients. This was Shukla's chance to keep both the money and the bag. After giving it deep thought, he decided that he would sell the second story to Ranjit.

Shukla was firm that he would keep the money underground near a jungle which was located outside Mussoorie. So, he dug a small piece of land, perfect for two suitcases to be fitted. He covered it with soil and marked it by planting a rubber plant.

•

Shukla reached Ranjit's house late that night. Ranjit was worried about Rahul. Shukla went to Ranjit and told him about what happened in Delhi. He said that the shooters at gunpoint took away both the bags and killed Jay in front of him.

Ranjit was shocked to hear about Jay's death. He told Shukla that he would find out from his sources what happened and who did it.

Later that night, Ranjit dialled a few numbers to know what had really happened. He got the news that Jay was killed in his shop in the morning and shooters were killed as they were trying to run away. They shot him and ran away without any bags. Ranjit didn't tell Shukla that the shooters were dead. Instead, he told him that the police was investigating the shooters. Ranjit was an old player in this game; he had a hunch that Shukla was hiding something from him.

"Do you know what was in the bag Shukla, which you took to Delhi?" Ranjit asked.

Shukla said, "No sir, I don't know what was in the bag."

"It has the finest marijuana. We harvest it in the jungle nearby. Now do you know how much was the loss when you gave the suitcase to these shooters," Ranjit asked Shukla in a polite voice.

"No sir, I don't know about it," Shukla replied.

"The loss is around one-crore rupees. Have you seen such huge money before?" Ranjit asked.

"No sir," Shukla started to stammer.

"This much of money is tough to hide." Ranjit chuckled and continued, "I hope whoever has my money and the drugs gets caught. It's difficult to trade these things in this business," Ranjit told Shukla.

When Shukla left, Ranjit called someone and asked him to keep an eye on Shukla.

•

Pandit was looking at the FIR copy given by Vishal. He noted that there was a driver mentioned who was driving Jagan's car that day. There was nothing written about it in the report. He was surprised to see why Brajesh never insisted to name that driver in this FIR report.

Pandit thought that he would speak to people who know this driver. He decided that he would start from the garage near Brajesh's place and speak to people if they knew anything about this driver. While he was going out, he changed his plan. He wanted to meet the fruit seller and see if he had come back from the city.

Pandit went to his house. When he reached there, he could hear a lot of laughter coming from the house.

He knocked at the door and a woman came out. Pandit asked to meet the fruit seller. At first, she hesitated, saying that he was not at home, but he insisted.

Listening to the conversation, a man came out. He looked at Pandit and said, "My name is Ram Kumar; I am the fruit seller you are looking for. Tell me what you want from me."

Pandit asked Ram to tell him what happened that day.

"I was going back home early that day, having sold all the fruit. So, the basket was empty and I was riding fast. Then I saw a truck coming in front of me, which was driving zigzag, as if the driver had lost control over the steering wheel. At first, it seemed that he was trying to save the van which was in front of him, but that didn't look right. Because the van went to the side of the truck. I stopped my bicycle immediately and got down from the road near the mountain. Unfortunately, that truck hit a car ahead and it got dashed into a tree and stopped.

"Then, two men came out of the van and saw the truck driver. The truck driver was unconscious. They checked him and went back to the car that had been hit. One of the men entered the car, and after a few minutes, he came out. After that, both the men pushed the car down the hill. They both looked around; it looked like they were checking if someone had seen them doing this. Then, they sat in the van and ran away.

"All this happened within a few minutes. I was hiding behind the big rock and saw all of this. After those two men drove away in the van, I took my bicycle and rushed back home in shock. At the same spot a few days later, I noticed that some policemen had kept barriers to inquire about the accident. I went to them and told them the entire story."

"And what about that small boy? Did you see him?" Pandit asked.

"Which small boy?" Ram Kumar asked him.

"That eight-year-old boy, who is the second eye witness in this case. Did you see him there?" Pandit asked Ram.

"Sir, there was no one other than me when this accident happened. I was alone on the road. I can swear on my child. There was no one!" Ram Kumar emphasised.

"The driver, did he try to run away? Try to remember, Ram!" Pandit asked.

"No sir, he was unconscious in the truck. His head was on the steering."

"Did you see how many people were in the car?" Pandit asked anxiously.

"There was an old man who was driving the car. He might be in his sixties," Ram Kumar replied.

"Are you telling me the truth Ram? Is this what you told to police also?" Pandit asked him in an authoritative voice.

"Why would I lie to you, sir? After I reported the incident to the police, two people came to my house. They said that they would give me a good job in Delhi and asked me to leave this city. The only condition was that I would have to come here at the end of every month to report at the police station. They are nice men sir. They helped me a lot to get a decent job."

Pandit was shocked to hear Ram's story. He recalled that there was nothing of this sort mentioned in the FIR report which Vishal gave. He took Ram's phone number, in case he needed to talk to him in future.

Next, Pandit decided to meet the small boy again to verify the story. When he reached their house, he asked, "Where are your kids? I met them a few days back here?"

The man said, "What are you saying? We just got married two days back."

Pandit was shocked. He asked again, "Then where is the family who used to stay here? I meet them a few days back."

"I am living here for the last ten years sir, which family are you talking about?"

Pandit was thoroughly confused now. But, the man continued, "But one person came here last week asking if he could get this house for a few days. He paid a good amount, so I agreed."

Pandit was sure now that someone had manipulated the information in the FIR and the story told by the boy was a pure bluff. Now, it was difficult to decide who was telling the truth. Dejected at having been misled this way, he went back to the hotel. There, he received the call from Brajesh.

"How are you doing, my friend? Looks like you are enjoying Mussoorie a lot. Come tonight, we will have dinner and drinks at my place."

"Let's meet! It has been long that I got a free drink from you," Pandit chuckled.

20

The Adrenaline Rush

When I woke up that day, I was still tired. Somehow, I got up from the bed and started to get ready for college. I plugged in my earphones and started walking. Suddenly, I heard the sharp noise of a car's breaks. I turned and saw a car coming towards me at a great speed. I tried to show him both of my hands to stop, but in a jiffy, I got hit.

Sometime later, I woke up and found myself in a bed. I looked up and saw a beautiful ceiling, with a chandelier hanging on it. The cushion was so soft, and the bed was so cozy that I had to push myself to come out, and still could not do it. That's when I felt a sharp pain in my left hand.

Someone said, "Are you okay now? Is your arm hurting?"

I looked at him and said, "There is a sharp pain, but I am unable to see what happened to me."

"I also don't know. Sir brought you here. He asked me to inform him once you wake up," the person replied.

He went outside the room and I gazed in the same direction. It was a huge glass instead of the wall. Outside, there was a big garden with a lot of beautiful plants.

"How are you feeling now?" a man asked me.

He told me that while he was driving back home, he accidentally hit me when I was crossing the road. I looked at my left hand; it was swollen. The doctor told him that there is no fracture and the swelling would remain, but it should be gone in the next couple of weeks after taking some medicines and rest.

"Why don't you stay here till you get well? I have a family doctor, and my servants will take care of you," he told me.

"Thanks, but I have to go back home. Trivedi will be worried about me. Where is my phone?" I asked him.

"It is here. Trivedi called and I told him that you are here and fine. So, don't worry about him," he said.

"Still, I will go back. I will feel more comfortable at my home." I insisted.

"If you really want to, I won't stop you. I will pay for all your medicines and doctor visits. Give me your phone number," he said.

I gave him my phone number and requested if he could drop me home.

He agreed and said, "I want to help you in any way I can. What is your name?" He asked.

"I am Arvind, people call me Aru. If you want to pay me, then please give me some work."

"Aru, you are a very good person. Tell me, what would you like to do? Your hand is swollen so much." He was curious to know what I could do.

"I saw your garden. It's so beautiful. Can I water your plants every morning?" I requested.

"Absolutely, no problem! I want you to start the work from tomorrow onwards then. Till you get well, you can come here and water the plants. For now, my family doctor has given a few medicines. Take all of them with you. I will also give some fruits to you," he said.

His driver drove me back to my house. When I got down, I asked him, "I didn't ask the name of the house owner. He is your boss, right? What is his name?"

"You don't know him? Looks like you are new in Mussoorie. He is Brajesh Thakur, the famous timber businessman in Mussoorie."

•

Trivedi was not at home so I took my medicine and went to sleep. Trivedi came home late at night; he was surprised to see me. He thought that I would stay at Brajesh Thakur's house for today, but I told him that I had insisted on coming back home. I also informed him that I had got a job to water plants at his house.

"Aru, in this condition, will you be able to water the plants? Are you serious?" Trivedi sounded frustrated.

"What's the problem! I have my right hand working and that is enough. And look at the positive side! I got a job and it will help me to sponsor my career requirements. And my Aai says—" Trivedi stopped me in between.

"Okay, I got your point. I know you will not take a break from the canteen." I nodded my head.

"Fine, then at least stop working at home. Shukla and I will cook food for you," Trivedi said and went to the kitchen.

•

Pandit went to Brajesh's house for dinner and drinks.

"Did you see Vishal's report?" Brajesh asked.

"Yeah, I saw, but it looks like all the evidences are pretty clear to him. But still, no arrest has been made. I wonder why?" Pandit said in a surprised voice.

"By now, you would have realized why there has been no arrest. You know that the truck belongs to Jay Chandra and I am sure you know that he is close to Ranjit. That clearly indicates who is behind all this," Brajesh told Pandit.

"But that truck was stolen a week before the incident."

"You believe that story, Pandit! Who will steal from a criminal like Jay Chandra?"

Pandit had started to feel that Ranjit might be influencing the case and had some benefit from Jagan's death. But he didn't have any strong evidence to support it.

"I note that point Brajesh, but what benefit would Ranjit get from Jagan uncle's death?" Pandit frowned.

"Ranjit wants to grow his business. He had some special interest in the timber business or something to do with the forest, and lately he was meeting with papa on this matter very frequently. My father was a simple and honest man who never thought that Ranjit would try to get into his business and export.

"Papa looked like he was upset with Ranjit, before his death. He told me many times that Ranjit was not agreeing to what he was asking him to do. I didn't understand what dad meant at that time. But after his death, the evidence clearly indicated that Ranjit had killed him for his own benefit," Brajesh said and went to the bar to make another drink.

"Do you mean that Ranjit is also in the timber business?" Pandit asked curiously.

"He is doing some sort of export business which involves him taking special interest in the forest, near Mussoorie," Brajesh told.

"Is it the same forest from where Jagan uncle was returning when he met with the accident?" Pandit asked.

"Yeah, the same jungle. He was cutting and exporting some kinds of trees about which I don't know much. See if you can find it out," Brajesh asked Pandit to look into it.

Pandit was clear now that the land of weed could be a common interest for both Ranjit and Jagan. Perhaps Ranjit ousted Jagan by getting him killed.

By the end of their meeting, Pandit was convinced that Ranjit was the person behind Jagan's death.

•

The next day, a car came and took me to Brajesh's house. After an hour of work, his family doctor came and saw me. He wrapped another bandage on my arm and told me not to take any load on this hand. After staying there for an hour, the car dropped me back to college.

I got down from the car and started to walk inside the college gate. A scooter honked from behind. I turned around and saw that she was on the scooter.

"Have you started a new business? Have you become a part-time hooligan, beating people around? If you don't want to talk to me, it's your choice. I always treated you as a good friend and I have the complete right to ask what happened to you?" She told me while sitting on the scooter.

"I met with an accident yesterday. Now I am fine and I can take care of myself. Don't worry, you can come to the canteen anytime. The canteen boy is still working round the clock to serve tea," I said and walked inside the college gate towards the canteen.

Prof Mishra's lecture was around 2 p.m. I told Trivedi that I have to be there outside the lecture. So, I went to class and served Prof Mishra tea and stood outside. He taught for an hour and at the end of the lecture, he said, "I have written a problem on the board. This is not that difficult, everyone please try to solve it. Submit your code to me via e-mail." He finished and came out. I was standing there, listening to Prof Mishra.

I quickly went to the board and saw the problem. I could solve half of it there in my mind, but it was tricky in the second half. So I came back to the canteen, thinking about it.

Later that night, I went to bed, but I was not able to sleep. Suddenly, something struck in my mind and I pulled out a paper from below the table and started to write the code. After two hours, finally, I managed to solve it.

I thought I should tell Prof Mishra that I have solved the problem, by writing answer on the board. I quickly got up, took Shukla's jacket, and ran towards the college. The college gate was closed and security guards were sitting at the gate. I wanted to get in. That was the only time when I could write the answer below the board without anyone noticing me.

I remembered that when I was walking to the auditorium a couple of weeks back, I had noticed a broken section of the boundary wall, which was being repaired. So I decided to try my luck.

I sneaked in through the small gap to reach the backside of the college. It was slightly dark. The streetlights were on. Then, I went to the floor near the board. The question was still there. I started to write the steps on how to solve it and also the key function which will be used in the code. I kept it small so that only Prof Mishra could understand the answer.

At the end of the answer, I wrote *Aru*. Then I thought that if I used my real name, people might know my true identity, so I wiped it again.

So, I wrote *Arvind* but there was not enough space to write my full name.

Finally, I thought of keeping it very short and decided to write *A.I.*, which were my initials. A pleasant smile spread across my face.

•

The next morning, the car came to take me to Brajesh's house. Usually, Brajesh wasn't up by that time, but he was awake and talking to someone in the garden that day. They were sitting on the garden swing and talking about someone who ran away from the site.

"The suitcase was not there. It was not taken by either Ranjit or those guys," he said worried.

"Even Ranjit doesn't have it. Can you confirm this?" Brajesh asked him curiously.

"Yeah, I know from my sources. His driver told him that both the guys took it away from him on gunpoint," the guy said.

"It's possible that the driver may be telling the truth," Brajesh said.

"The police investigated that car which was burnt after the accident; there was nothing apart from two bodies," he said.

"Do you think Shukla has it?" Brajesh asked in suspicion.

I was just a few metres away from them, watering the plant. I heard the name Shukla and a few words by which I could figure out the context.

"Yes, I am sure it's with Shukla. I am keeping an eye on him. As soon as I get something, I will call you," he said.

"Keep me informed," Brajesh told this guy. After that, he left the place and Brajesh was alone on the swing thinking about it.

After finishing my work at Brajesh's house, I went to college. From far, I could see a crowd standing near the board on which Prof Mishra had written that question. Instead of going to the canteen, I walked to the board to see what the noise was about. Everyone was murmuring "A.I."

After a while, I saw Prof Mishra walking towards the board. The crowd dispersed to let Prof Mishra see the answer. He looked at it and said to himself, "It is correct!" He was astonished to see such a fast response. Everyone started to clap. It was the first time in the history of MJK that Prof Mishra's question received the correct response in a day.

He looked around and asked, "Who did it? Who is A.I. here? Come, show me your face." He took a pause and repeated, "Anyone here, no one? Find out who did this and ask him to come and meet me in the cabin." And he walked away.

I was extremely thrilled. That moment was the happiest moment of my life. I reached the canteen with a smile. That whole day in the canteen, students were gossiping about "A.I." I never knew that my initials would become so popular.

What an irony! I was given two names at different points of my life. When I was humiliated in front of everyone by Andre, I was called 'Shortcut' and when I solved the problem; I was recognized by the name A.I.

The only difference was that when I was humiliated, people saw me; but when I was praised, they didn't. These two were the most defining moments of my life.

Someone has rightly said, "Work hard in silence and let success make all the noise."

The last lecture of Prof Mishra was an hour before college ended. I went upstairs and attended his lecture, standing outside the door. At the last moment, when the lecture was about to end, Prof Mishra came out of the class suddenly and saw me standing at the door, I saw him and quickly scooted away. He looked puzzled about what I was doing there. He told the class that he would start the next programming language 'R programming', from next week onwards. I heard him and decided to start the free lectures online on R programming.

I was desperately feeling the need for a computer or a laptop now. It was getting a bit tricky to write the code on paper and see if that would work on not. Also, I thought that having a laptop would increase my efficiency to learn. I thought of calling Aai and asking her if she could provide me with some money. I had also saved some from my salary. But then, I dropped the idea, thinking that it was unfair on my part to burden her. I decided that I would arrange for it somehow.

I told Trivedi about the laptop,

He said, "Why don't you ask Brajesh? He is a rich man. Get some money from him on credit and promise to return it back."

I liked Trivedi's idea of asking Brajesh. I decided I would seek his help.

•

In the morning, I was at Brajesh's house. After watering the plants, I waited for Brajesh to come out. A few minutes later, Brajesh came out and asked me what happened. He took me with him and asked me to sit on the swing. I told Brajesh everything about my learning and how keen I was to pick up computer programming as my career goal.

He was listening to me carefully. After I finished he said, "Aru, the way you are living your life reminds me of my dad. He worked hard. He was honest, he loved people, and he supported everyone he met in his life. He started from nothing and brought us here. And one unfaithful day, god took him away from us." He paused and took a deep breath and continued.

"When I talk to you, it makes me feel that I am looking at my father's childhood. I will pay you for your laptop. I know no matter how much I convince you that you don't have to pay the money back, you will not listen because of the principles your Aai has taught you. But I need you to promise me. You will come here regularly. I want to see you every day. Each day when I see you, it seems that I am looking at the struggle of my father. So promise me that you will work here even after you get well."

I nodded my head in agreement. I got my first laptop that day. Brajesh took me to the store and bought one for me. The next thing I wanted to do was to install all the free software that I could learn.

I spent the whole evening installing the free software and enrolling in free classes. It gave me such an adrenaline rush!

21

The Rubik's Cube Problem

Pandit was convinced that the FIR copy had false information. He wanted to know exactly what happened that day so he went to the accident spot to see if he could get any more clues.

The case was almost a couple of years old, and it was difficult to find any evidence at the spot. He decided that he would go to the police station where the case was registered and try to get as much information as possible. He found that the police station near Janpad had registered the FIR. He went in to report the loss of his wallet.

While sitting there, he saw a few constables sitting around there and joking with each other. Pandit managed to befriend one of the constables. He took him out of the police station and asked him if he could help him in exchange of money. He hesitated slightly, but after sometimes, he agreed.

"I want you to give me the original FIR copy of Jagan Thakur's accident case. I also want to know what exactly happened that day. Can you help me?" Pandit asked.

"Look boss, I will give you the FIR copy. But no one knows the truth. We rely on the information given by Ram Kumar. Other than that, the story of that boy that you mentioned is correct, but no one knows where that came from. Vishal sir signed the FIR and that was final," he replied.

Pandit paid some money to the constable and told him not to tell anyone about his visit, especially Vishal.

The constable gave a copy of the FIR to Pandit. After reading the complete FIR, he was convinced that Ram Kumar's story was correct. But there was no mention of someone getting down from the van and going inside the car. Someone has botched up the FIR report. Even though Ram Kumar was right, they never recorded his correct statement. The next task for Pandit was to find out who was in the van. And the only person who could help him was Ram Kumar.

As Pandit was in the police station, he went inside to find Vishal's picture somewhere. There were pictures of a couple of inspectors who had been awarded the best service in that quarter; Vishal was one of them. Pandit quietly took out his camera and snapped his picture on his phone.

He decided that he would go to Ram Kumar and ask him if he had seen this guy. Probably he could give him some clue.

It was late evening when Pandit called Ram. He was at the Picture Palace bus station from where he was to catch a bus for Delhi. Pandit asked him to wait but Ram said that he would have to board the bus in a few minutes.

So Pandit rushed on his scooter to meet Ram. When he reached there, the bus had left the station. Pandit saw Ram sitting on the window seat; he followed the bus, overtook it, and asked the driver to stop it.

The driver shouted at Pandit, "Are you mad? If you want to die, go and find another bus." Pandit rushed inside the bus and showed the picture to Ram.

Ram said, "He is the guy who came that day to my home. And gave me the offer to work in Delhi."

"Are you sure Ram? Please, can you look closely?" Pandit insisted.

"I am sure sir. He was the one who came to my house," Ram confirmed.

•

Shukla's behaviour changed in the house after he came from Delhi. He remained quiet most of the time. He used to get scared easily. Sometimes, when he was in deep sleep, he used to wake up at night shouting, "No, no! Don't kill me."

Trivedi and I were getting very worried about Shukla. What came to my mind was the discussion that Brajesh was having with that guy in his house.

Is there something that Shukla is hiding from me? I needed to find out.

•

As usual, I tracked Prof Mishra's lecture in college regularly now. He asked the class about who A.I. was, but he did not get any answer. That day he decided to put up another question on the board. He told the class that he wants to see who can answer that as this time he had given a more challenging question compared to the students of that grade.

The problem was to solve a Rubik's cube given specific patterns of colours on all the sides; the patterns were provided in a text file format.

The program was supposed to take the input from that file, process it, and generate the steps a user should make to solve that cube. I had seen a Rubik's cube before, but never solved it in my life. So, after college, I went to Mall Road and bought one from the toy store.

I also decided to start working as a freelancer, now that I had a hang of programming languages. So, immediately I texted Pandit and asked, "Can we meet tomorrow? I need to ask you about the freelancer thing." He responded and agreed to help me.

I tried to play around the Rubik's cube but it was difficult, as it required both the hands to play. I noticed that swelling in my hand had come down a lot but there was still pain which was not subsiding.

When I woke up the next morning, Trivedi was asleep, but Shukla was awake that day. He was standing outside the house in that foggy morning.

I went out and spoke to him, "Is everything is okay with you, Shukla? Nowadays, you wake up in the night, shouting. Please tell us if there is something with which we can help you."

Shukla was quiet. And I continued, "If you are worried about that gloves matter, please tell me. I will speak to him. I haven't told you about my meeting with that guy. What he said is that he doesn't have an answer right now. But he promised me that he will help you in the case with whatever best he can."

"What's happening Aru? Are you meeting someone to discuss if I am in trouble" Shukla said in an exasperated tone.

I said, "Shukla, you know all the answers to all these questions. Talk to me. Trivedi and I are like family. We will help you."

"What will you guys do? Nothing! It is better that I handle all this myself. When I helped that guy bring the truck back to Mussoorie, that one incident changed my life forever," Shukla said in a worried voice.

"Which truck, Shukla? Tell us what happened?" Trivedi came out from the room and asked Shukla.

Shukla shook his head in frustration and went back inside the house. Brajesh's driver was at the door, honking for me to come inside the car.

I told Trivedi, "Please talk to him; something is not right."

•

At Brajesh's house, the doctor came and looked at my hand. He told us that there might be some problem in the wrist. We would need to do an x-ray to find out. He asked me not to use that hand and keep it steady.

That was troubling news because while using the laptop, I was moving my hand a lot. And I had to solve the Rubik's cube problem by any means. The best way was to pretend that the pain was not that much and I would wait for a couple of days before doing an x-ray.

Later that day, I meet Pandit at Mall Road to have dinner. He had this pre-condition that I would not ask about how the investigation was going. I told him that I had a new job at some businessman's house and he paid for my laptop on credit. And now I needed to try my hand in freelancing to earn some extra bucks.

Pandit told me that there were a few famous sites where I could register myself. I was listening carefully to each of the steps that he told me. At the end of the conversion, I asked him," Pandit, do you know about Rubik's cube? Can you solve it?"

"Yes, I can solve it within five minutes. I was the best among my college friends," he said proudly.

I insisted him to show me how it was done and he agreed.

When he dropped me at my home, I went in and brought the Rubik's cube with me. He looked at it and gave me his watch, asking me to see how long he took. I could see the movement and steps he took. I was trying to figure out what exactly he was thinking while solving it. After he finished, I saw the watch. It had been four minutes and thirty-five seconds. I was amazed to see how quickly he had solved it.

He started the scooter and asked me, "Is everything okay with Shukla? He is around, right?"

I told him about Shukla's concerning behaviour.

Pandit said, "Aru, don't let him know anything right now, but it seems that he is not guilty in the case on which I am working. For now, keep it with you. He has been framed. As there is no evidence of him being innocent right now, I can't do anything if he gets caught. It's just a matter of him being recognized by someone that he was driving that truck. Sooner or later, things will change. So, don't worry!"

I was relieved to hear that Shukla was innocent, but it was important to know what Shukla was hiding from us.

•

I logged in to freelancer.com, the website Pandit had told me about. The steps were fairly easy to register. I looked at a couple of projects and bid on a few with the quote that I would charge for the work. I closed the site and went back to solve the Rubik's cube. It took me around an hour to solve it for the first time. The next one, I solved in forty minutes. In the next three hours, I had solved the cube five times. Then I started to look at the pattern and look at the best algorithm to solve it. I had already downloaded the Python and R programs on my laptop, so I started writing the code.

After a few minutes, Shukla came home. He was quiet as usual. He told Trivedi that he has some work and had also brought Ranjit's SUV with him. He would go out for a couple of hours and come back. I don't know why, but he spoke very suspiciously. Shukla had never done this before.

As soon as he went into the washroom, I got up and looked outside. I could see that the SUV was parked just outside our house. I told Trivedi that I was going for a walk and would be back soon.

Shukla had kept the SUV keys in the room. Before leaving home, I swiftly went to the keys and quietly clicked the button to unlock the SUV. I went out and opened the boot of the SUV and sat inside.

I waited for almost thirty minutes, after which I heard the SUV being locked and unlocked again. Shukla came and drove the SUV from there. I was looking from the rear glass to see where he was going. I faintly remembered that this was the route towards the Kempty Falls. After driving for a few minutes, we crossed the waterfall spot and stopped at a lonely place in the forest.

Shukla parked the SUV and went to one rubber plant. To my surprise, he just stood there. I came out of the boot and sauntered towards the direction where Shukla had gone.

It was pitch dark. I switched on the phone torchlight and looked around. I couldn't see Shukla anywhere. I slowly walked over the leaves but suddenly; I started to feel choked by an arm that gripped my neck.

I tried to speak, "Wait... Wait..."

The man holding my neck said, "Who are you? What are you doing here?"

"Shukla, it's me, Aru, leave me!" I tried to speak in a choked voice. And he removed his hand from my neck.

"Aru? What the hell are you doing here?" Shukla came in front of me.

I started to cough, and he patted at my back to make me comfortable. It took me a few minutes to be normal. I looked at Shukla and said, "You almost killed me."

"I am sorry, I thought someone was following me," Shukla replied.

"Why are you so worried nowadays? What happened to you? I came here, hiding in your SUV, to find out what is going on in your life. Can you tell me why you are here?" I shouted at Shukla.

Shukla took me to that rubber plant and started digging. After a few minutes, he reached the bags. He showed those two bags to me, one was packed with two-thousand rupee notes and the other had black packets. He told me the complete story of his encounter with Jay Chandra.

Shukla and I were sitting near the hole, looking at the bags. I told Shukla, "You should tell Ranjit. If you tell the truth to him, he will spare you, but if you hide and he finds out that you have kept these bags here, then you know what will happen," I told Shukla.

"I have worked with Ranjit for many years. The only thing he doesn't like is someone betraying him. No matter how big or small it is, he has only one answer to it. Kill him."

He took a deep breath and continued in a low voice, "But, he will not be able to figure out that I have these bags. Because I am the only one who knows about the transportation of marijuana, and I am the only one who does this for him."

"That black bag contains marijuana! You mean drugs?" I was appalled.

Shukla nodded his head.

"I don't think nobody knows about this. I know people are talking about these bags," I said in suspicion.

"What are you saying? No one knows about this, apart from Ranjit and me."

"No, that's not correct Shukla. I heard someone speaking about you and this bag. They were saying that these bags were not with someone called Jay or with Ranjit. And they are keeping an eye on you. I am sure they will be able to track you."

I was worried and continued, "The only way to come out of this is by telling the truth to Ranjit. You have been loyal to him. He may throw you out of the job, but you will still be alive," I told Shukla.

"No way! I am not going to tell him the truth, and neither will you. He will kill me for sure." Shukla was worried.

Shukla's decision to hide the bags was a disaster. I didn't know what to do apart from supporting the truth. That is what my Aai had taught me. Sometimes, it is difficult to accept the truth. But, that is the only path that leads to a peaceful life.

Shukla and I came back to our house, and Shukla made me promise that I won't tell anyone about this, not even Trivedi. When we walked into the house, Trivedi looked at both of us and said, "Where were you both? I was waiting for you outside, and two people came and asked about you. Who are they?"

Shukla and I looked at each other and understood that we were being followed.

Shukla replied, "For both of us? I don't know anyone."

I went back to my desk and opened my laptop. I had got the first response for a bid job. If I finished his code, I would be paid ten thousand rupees. I accepted that job. I picked my phone and texted Pandit.

I got my first freelancing project.

You rock, Aru! Best of luck! was his instant response.

22

The New Actor

On the other side of the city, Pandit followed Vishal and made a note of all the people he met. While he was tracking him, Vishal never met Ranjit or Brajesh, even once. Nor did he meet any of their staff. Pandit was noting down the names of people and their locations. He tried to draw some common connection between them, but there was nothing. It was an exhausting exercise to keep hiding from Vishal and following him. Finally, Pandit walked out of his room and started to roam around his hotel garden to take a break from all this.

While he was walking around, a waiter came running to him. He gave Pandit his scooter keys and said, "Sir, I think it fell from your pocket. It was lying in the lobby, sir."

Pandit thanked him and took the keys. But he was curious to know how he had managed to find that these were his keys. So he called the waiter and asked him how he knew that these keys belonged to my scooter.

"Sir, one day, you were at reception waiting for a car to pick you up. When you went out of the hotel, you forgot the scooter keys at the reception. It had this nice design on it. That lady at the reception remembered it. I went to your room; you were not there. I even checked at the scooter, but you were not there. So, I thought of giving it to you later," he said submissively.

Pandit smiled and kept the keys in the pocket. Then a thought came to his mind.

Why don't I use this trick for Vishal and see where he goes?

•

Pandit went to the reception and took the printout of the gloves on an A4-sized paper and wrote something on it. Then, he took the scooter and went to Vishal's house. When he reached there, he saw that the door was closed, but the lights were on. There was someone in the house. He put that printout in an envelope, kept it at Vishal's door, rang the bell and went swiftly outside the gate. He hid behind the trees and waited for Vishal to come out.

Vishal opened the door and saw the envelope. He opened it and read:

I have the gloves and the eye witness. But it will not reach the court because I know this evidence is fake.

Vishal took the letter and came out of the house. He looked around, but I was hiding well. He seemed to be frustrated and went inside.

Pandit was patiently waiting for Vishal to come out of the house and meet someone. Pandit stood there for an hour, but nothing happened. Finally, just when Pandit was giving up and thinking of what to do, Vishal came out of the house, took his bike and went away. Pandit followed him.

Vishal was worried that if anyone found out that the evidence had been planted, the whole game would fall apart. Finally, he reached a big bungalow. Pandit parked his scooter outside the house, far from the gate. Once Vishal was inside the house, Pandit went close and saw the name outside the house.

It was written, 'Bhandari.'

Pandit had never heard this name before. If Vishal had gone to meet Bhandari about the envelope, then Bhandari was the new character in the story.

Pandit stood outside Bhandari's house a few metres away from the main gate. He dialled Brajesh and asked, "Hey, how do you know Vishal? Why did you give me Vishal's contact for this case?"

"He was investigating the case and looked honest to me," Brajesh replied.

"What made you trust him more than anyone? There should be something. Tell me, Brajesh!"

"What happened, Pandit? It looks like you are questioning me. Why are you so worried?"

"Brajesh, you have to be honest with me if you want me to handle this case. What made you think that Vishal is an honest man and is not influenced by Ranjit?" Pandit asked Brajesh.

"Because he was investigating—" Brajesh was stopped in between by Pandit.

"No, because *he* told you that *he* knows Ranjit is behind all this. And he will collect all the evidence and frame him," Pandit said.

"Yes," Brajesh replied.

"And who is Bhandari?" Pandit asked in suspicion.

"Deepak Bhandari is a small businessman, who arrived in Mussoorie a few years back. I don't know much about him," Brajesh said.

"Brajesh, I can tell you one thing. I am not sure whether Ranjit is involved in this or not, but Bhandari is a key player in this case. It would be better for you to tell me if you know anything about him."

"Pandit, trust me! I don't know much about Bhandari. We have met only twice, that's it. I don't have any personal connection with him," Brajesh said, trying to convince Pandit.

Pandit said that he would get more information and call him back.

When Pandit was reaching for his scooter, he saw Vishal coming out from Bhandari's house. He again followed him. Vishal then went to Ranjit's house. Pandit stayed there, waiting for Vishal. It took almost three hours for him to come out.

Now, Pandit was sure that at least two people were involved in this case – Bhandari and Ranjit.

23

Eklavya

I was eager to finish my first freelancing project. So, I thought of parking the Rubik's problem aside and finish my first assignment. That night, I worked till late to finishing that job.

After midnight, Shukla woke up and came to me. "Today is Trivedi's birthday. Come, let's wake him up."

We slowly went to Trivedi and wished him, "Happy birthday!" We even went out to celebrate his birthday. We sat in a small café where we ordered cake, drinks and chips. Trivedi cut the cake, and we all sang the birthday song for him. Aunty, who seemed to be the owner of the café, joined us in our small celebration.

After a few minutes, when we were winding up, I asked aunty, "You kept the shop open so late! Does anyone come here? It is open for twenty-four hours, but I hardly see anyone right now."

"Yes, son. Only a few people know about the shop. Only they come here," she replied.

"The cake was fantastic! Are these homemade?" I asked.

"Yes, all cakes here are homemade," she replied.

"Then you should promote these cakes. Why don't you do that?" I asked.

"How can I? I don't have much money to invest; probably one day I will find a way to advertise about them," she replied.

"Okay aunty, let me shoot a small video with you, saying how much I liked this cake," I replied and she agreed.

I shot the one-minute video with her and sent it to Pandit. I also told him that if he was hungry, and there was no place to go around midnight, he should come to aunty's place. She had made a fabulous cake for us. I thanked aunty and came out and started walking towards our house. After a few minutes, Pandit replied.

Hey that looks great.Your video makes it more interesting to visit the place.

That night, after going back home, I finished my first assignment and submitted the codes.

•

The next morning, when I went to Brajesh, I saw a police motorbike standing in front of the gate. I heard Brajesh shouting at someone in a happy tone, saying that it is excellent news. They had finally found the evidence against the truck driver.

Then, Brajesh came out with someone and dropped him off on his motorbike. While going back inside the house, he saw me and smiled.

I was able to connect the dots now. Shukla *was* the truck driver.

•

The Rubik's cube problem was yet to be solved. I decided to go to the canteen with my Rubik's cube so that I am able to give it more time. While walking, I was so engrossed in solving the cube that I bumped someone and my rubik's cube fell from my hand.

"I am sorry," I said. I quickly picked up the cube and continued with it. I didn't see who the person was.

When I reached the counter, Trivedi told me that Prof Mishra had come in to say that he wanted a cup of tea during his lecture. I nodded my head and got to work.

That day, after a long time, she came to the canteen. When I saw her, she looked depressed and lost. I thought that might be because I was being too harsh on her. After all, it was my fault that I expected too much from her.

I thought of talking to her that day. I poured a cup of tea and went to her table. She looked at me, and went out. I was baffled by her response and wanted to know what was going on in her life.

I reached outside the class where Prof Mishra was going to conduct his lecture. I was standing outside, listening to him. But again, at the end of the lecture, Prof Mishra opened the class gate suddenly and saw me standing outside. I looked at him and scooted from there.

That day, I had a sequence in my mind to solve that Rubik's problem. I went back home, opened my laptop and started working. I was so absorbed in my work that Trivedi didn't disturb me.

Later in the night, it was dinner time and Trivedi asked me to eat. The food was there on my plate, and I didn't even look at it. Around 9 p.m., I started to run the regression program. It failed. I tried again around 10 p.m. It failed again.

At last, around 11 p.m., I ran the program again, checking all the issues. It ran successfully. I changed the input, executed it again, and it finished again successfully. Around midnight, I ran it for one last time, with the worst-case parameters combination, and it ran successfully again.

Finally, I had solved the Rubik's problem which Prof Mishra had written on the board!

I got up from my seat and ran towards the college. The gate was closed, so I went to the back side, and through the gap in the wall, I reached the college building. I went up to the second floor and reached the board. I couldn't control my excitement. After all, I had finished the steps on how to solve the problem, what algorithms are required, and the R and Python packages that needed to be used. After completing my answer, I signed it A.I.

I looked at the board one last time, chuckled, and said, "Yes!"

"Stop there!" A loud voice echoed on the floor.

I stopped. I thought probably the guards had seen me. I turned back and looked at the person who was standing in the lobby.

He was Prof Mishra, with a torch in his hand. He shouted again.

"Who are you? Come here? Are you AI? I knew that none of my college students could have solved this problem. I had a clue that some outsider is coming here at odd hours to solve this. Since the day I wrote this problem on the board, I am sitting in my cabin, waiting for someone to come one day. And finally, you are here."

I was startled. He continued, "Don't hide. I have found you now. Come here. Else, I will call the guards."

Instead of me walking to Prof Mishra, he walked towards me. I stood quietly. He looked at the board and said, "This is absolutely correct! Did you do it yourself? Tell me."

I looked at him and said, "Yes, I did it myself."

He looked at me and said, "In the canteen, when you bumped into me and the Rubik's cube fell, I guessed that it might be you. I know you stand outside my class and listen to my lectures. So *the A.I* is the canteen boy. Am I right?"

"Yes sir."

"Did you solve this?"

"Yes sir."

"Then why didn't you tell me in the class? Why are you playing hide and seek?"

"Sir, I am already infamous in the college, and everyone calls me 'shortcut'. I couldn't dare to come forward."

"What does A.I. stand for?" He asked.

"It's my name, sir. Arvind Ingle," I said submissively.

"Haha!" Professor Mishra laughed.

He asked me to come with him to his cabin. He listened to my story as I told him how the definition of artificial intelligence had inspired me, how I had picked up programming, listened to his lectures and learned from online lectures.

"So, you are my Eklavya! But don't worry, I won't ask you for your thumb," Prof Mishra said. He was very impressed.

"Aru, I will teach you all about machine learning and AI. From now on, you will come every day to my house. I want you to master it. I want people to remember you as A.I."

That day, I met my guru – Prof Mishra.

•

Now, the college had a secret superhero A.I., who could solve any problem, and no one knew who he was. Students had different theories about him. Some believed that he was the spirit of a brilliant student who was roaming in the college and taking revenge by solving Prof Mishra's problems. Others believed that aliens were visiting college. Slowly, A.I. became the talk of the town.

While the other students were chatting animatedly, I saw her sitting at a table, away from all these stories, alone. I went to her table, kept the tea cup on it and said, "If it is I who made you sad, then I am very sorry."

She looked at me and smirked, "Do you think life is unfair only to you, Aru? Take a break! Look around, people have more serious problems than you."

"Do you want to share it with me?" I asked.

She stood up and started to walk out. I said in a little loud voice, "Sorry, I forgot, I am just a canteen boy and a shortcut. Why will you speak to me?"

She turned back, held my hand, and dragged me out of the canteen. Students saw me being dragged by her. She took me near to her scooter and hopped on. Then, she took it out from the stand and said, "Sit!"

I didn't move. She yelled, "I said, sit!" I was baffled by what had happened to her. She drove me to the Company Garden.

At Company Garden, we got down and walked towards a bench. She sat there and I followed her. A few minutes later, she looked at me and said, "Aru, my parents got separated when I was barely ten years old."

"My father and Ranjit uncle, Rahul's father, were school friends. I used to meet Rahul since then. Whenever my parents fought, I used to get scared with those loud screams. I was so depressed that I used to cry, sitting in some corner, all alone. One day I called Rahul. He tried his best to pacify me and made me smile. After that day, whenever my parents' fought, I called up Rahul. He never disappointed me. Later, he used to come to my house without letting anyone know.

"Slowly I started to ignore my parent's fight because I knew Rahul was there to take care of me. Imagine a small boy who understands you so much. After my parents got divorced, both my parents wanted my custody.

"Then one day, the judge asked me in the court whom I wanted to stay with. I said my grandmother. You know why? Because she stays in Mussoorie and I wanted to stay here so that I could meet Rahul whenever I wanted. Rahul and I are made for each other.

"He proposed to me to express his love. It was Rahul's birthday. He chose that day to be the most precious day when he wanted to propose to me. Usually, on Rahul's birthday, many friends visit him. But that year, he reserved it for me. Everything was going well, but suddenly, everything changed.

"A few days back, I went to his house. I saw him lying on his bed, looking so weak. I could see that he was not feeling well. I asked him what happened. Then, I got to know that his kidneys are not functioning properly. Both his kidneys could fail at any moment. If he doesn't find a donor soon, he wouldn't survive. I don't want him to die, Aru. I love him."

She took a pause and continued, "And you think that people calling you 'shortcut' is the worst that can happen. No Aru, one day you will leave Mussoorie, for good. You can start your life fresh. But what about Rahul? What about me? I don't want to lose him, Aru. I can't take it anymore."

I couldn't see the tears rolling down from her eyes, which she wiped with shivering hands.

I stood there and placed my hand on hers.

"It took you so long to tell me this. I thought you treated me like a good friend. And you could share anything you wanted with me."

She was quiet. I continued, "I am not sure how I could be of any help to you. But, please feel free to tell me whatever you want to share. This will take some burden off your shoulders. I can't take Rahul's place, but yes, I will always be your good friend."

She nodded her head and looked at me, "Aru, tell me one thing. You still don't know my name, right?" She questioned.

"No, I don't. And you know what, I don't want to know. I don't want to give a name to this pure friendship. Let it be like this – selfless, pristine and unnamed."

24

Building My Startup

Pandit was in his hotel, thinking about his next move to find out the reality of Jay's truck which was stolen. While he was sitting on his chair, thinking about it, he got a message on his phone from Brajesh.

Looks like, we have finally cracked the case.Vishal has got the evidence of who was driving the truck that day. He works for Ranjit. I will tell you as soon as I get more information about this case.

Pandit knew that Shukla would be framed now, after he dropped that envelope at Vishal's house. He had to find out the truth behind the truck. Most importantly, why did Vishal wait for so long to provide evidence that Shukla was driving the truck?

Pandit texted me that night.

Shukla may be in trouble soon. But I will do my best to take him out of it. Stay strong.

•

While all of this was happening around me, I started to go to Prof Mishra's house. He taught me all about data science, machine learning and AI concepts. Those sessions were creating more interest in me. Alongside, my freelancer job was picking up, as my first project landed me more jobs. I was falling short of time.

One day, while studying at Prof Mishra's house, I asked him if he knew the names of students in his class who were good at programming. He quizzed me on why I was asking him this question. I didn't want to hide anything from him and talked about my projects as a freelancer. Prof Mishra said he would speak to his students to check if they could support me.

I told Prof Mishra, "It would be better for students that they learn from real-life problems. I really want them to support my work. If I managed to bring all these intelligent brains together, then we could work and excel together."

"That's a good idea Aru. So you want to meet them? I will introduce you to them," he said.

It reminded me of being called a 'shortcut'. I said, "Sir, I wanted to keep my identity hidden. I want to work with them without introducing myself and without using my name."

Prof Mishra said, "But how will you work with them without them knowing you."

I told my plan to him step-by-step. He liked it and was convinced that I could run the project.

After my discussion with the professor, he asked a few of his students about these jobs. They agreed to do it.

Slowly, within a week, I had a team of five students who were working for me to write the code the way I wanted. Unknowingly, I was running a small startup with a few students. And during the day, as a canteen boy, I served tea to them.

•

Pandit was frustrated with the thought that Vishal was taking so much time to arrest Shukla. He could have done it with the help of a small boy, long ago. While he was in the hotel checking his mails, a notification popped up. He had received a new mail from Milan Singh. There was a word document attached to it. The phone rang simultaneously. He opened the document and also picked up the phone,

"Hello Pandit! Did you see my mail?"

"Just saw it. So, you managed to convert the script into English," Pandit asked him curiously.

"Yes, it's done. But I am worried, Pandit. There is something mysterious about the land and the temple. I haven't seen anything like this before in any Shaivism text so far," Milan said.

"Hold on. Make it simple for me, please. What it is?" Pandit was worried.

"Let me explain this in a very simple way, based on as much as I have understood the text. You know, long back Ravana prayed to Shiva to give him immortal powers to be alive for five million years."

"Yes," Pandit said.

Milan continued, "During that time when Ravana was praising lord Shiva, Shiva was busy with his devotees to bless them. You know Shiva is also called *Bholanath*, which means that he is so simple that anyone could make him happy and he would bless him with whatever he wanted. No matter who the devotees are, Shiva is pure at heart.

"One day a devotee called Tanah asked Shiva to bless him so that he could build a place where he could make Shiva stay for as many days as he wanted. He prayed to Shiva so that he could grow the finest cannabis. This is something Shiva liked the most.

"So, Shiva blessed him with a field of cannabis. He told Tanah that if he installed his statue in that field and prayed to him every day, he would always come and stay there whenever he wanted. Tanah came there and waited for Shiva to come down. He planted such wonderful cannabis that Shiva couldn't resist.

"Now, here is the twist! Shiva found out that when he stayed there in that field, the demons on earth were free to do whatever they wanted. He cursed Tanah, saying that if anyone grew cannabis in the field or took it out from that field, then someone close to that person would die. This made that finest cannabis cursed. The temple had a red ruby stone statue of Shiva.

"A few days before Shiva is supposed to come down to this statue, it starts emitting a red spectrum of light, a beautiful glow around it, indicating that Shiva is coming. It is slightly red at the beginning but becomes blood red when he is there. The whole field is drenched in red colour. The colour of blood!

"There is a calculation based on which we can estimate when Shiva will come on the field. I have managed to decode that. Listen, based on our calculation and *the* shloka mentioned in the script, the day for Shiva to arrive there next time is very soon. On that day, when Shiva is there in the field, the quality of cannabis is in its purest form. It's priceless. If you take out the cannabis that day and sell it in the market, you are sitting on treasure worth a billion dollars. This event happened around five thousand years ago when Shiva came last. If I go based on the shlokas and formula and calculate, then the next time Shiva will be there is very soon."

There was a moment of silence, when Pandit and Milan didn't speak. Milan asked, "Hello Pandit, are you there?"

"Yes," Pandit said in a low voice.

"What happened?" Milan asked

"This is a mystery, Milan. Are you sure this is what is written there?"

"Yes Pandit. Can I ask you something? From where did you get this script? Have you been to this place? Have you seen that statue of Shiva"?

"Yes, I have seen that place. I was there. What is the next date when this will happen, Milan?" Can you be more precise?

"Two months from now, Pandit. This day, it will be a full moon night. No stars will be seen in the sky and the night will be very long."

"Please Milan; can I get the specific date?" Pandit asked.

"I have to consult others to find out when exactly it will happen? Astrologers will be able to suggest the accurate date. I will text you once I find out," Milan said.

There was a lot in this case other than a murder. If the place is cursed for the people who stole the cannabis, then why would someone do that?

•

Brajesh was elated that finally, the case would be solved. His suspicion was right – Ranjit was behind the killing of his father.

He dialled Ranjit and said angrily, "I told you that I will prove that you are behind my father's death. Now, I have solid evidence, and soon we will build a concerted case against you. Now count your days Ranjit."

"I don't know what rubbish you are talking about, Brajesh. Jagan was my good friend. Even now I am fulfilling the obligation that he has left behind. What benefit did I have from killing him?" Ranjit said.

"What obligation? You were behind our timber business for a long time, Ranjit. You wanted to control that too. But when you failed to take it over, you killed my dad," Brajesh yelled.

"Shut up, Brajesh! If I would not have been around, Jagan would have died long back. But It's worthless to tell you all that." Ranjit replied and hung up the phone.

Then, Ranjit received a text message.

Two more to go. We want the second last consignment in the next one week. Hope you remember Jagan's promise.

He shook his head in disappointment and walked out of the room. He called on the number from which he had received the message and said, "Yes, I remember. I will bring the consignment myself this time."

25
The Truth

Gradually, I learnt a new programming language called Kotlin to develop mobile apps. It was quite exciting. The college students working with me and I had a chat group on the phone where we used to communicate with each other. My name was Ingle in the group. I appreciated the way they were helping me in my work. New projects were coming in and my income was rising steadily.

While working that day, I got an idea to build an app where people could share their recorded reviews of a restaurant online or be live to share their reviews. I pushed the task to our group chat as a new project by a client. Everyone liked it. I started to design the user interface for the application.

When I had heard about app development for the first time, I thought it was a crazy idea. I never realized that I could ever do it in my life. But now, I was building my own app. That day, I realize that we should never underestimate ourselves. Pandit's words echoed in my mind.

You know Aru, someone said once, it always seems impossible until it's done.

I gave the app development project a name, VoiceEat.

After I finished my work that day, I went to bed thinking about Shukla. He was not in the house and when Pandit said that he might be in trouble, I started to worry a lot about him. Finally, I decided that I would convince Shukla to tell Ranjit the truth and be safe, instead of hiding from him.

That day, Shukla came very late. I was awake when he walked in. I asked him to come out with me as I had something to share.

"Shukla, looks like there is some evidence the police has found against you. Can you tell me what happened that day? See, I know someone who can help you."

Shukla looked up and said, "I will tell you what happened that day."

•

Shukla's Story

That day, I was returning from my village to Mussoorie. In the bus, I met a driver, Ramesh Tiwari. Ramesh had boarded the bus from Delhi. He didn't have change for the ticket, so I gave him some money. He promised me that he would return it when we reached Mussoorie. He was working for one of the local businessmen here, Deepak Bhandari.

While we were on that bus, he received a call from Bhandari saying that his truck was in a garage a few kilometers before Mussoorie and asked him to get down at Asarori and drive it till Mussoorie. Ramesh asked me to join him so that he would have company till Mussoorie and when we reached, he would pay me my money back. I agreed. After sometime, we got down near Asarori where his truck was kept in the garage. While we were in the garage, Ramesh got another phone call informing him that his mother was severely ill. He had to go back to Delhi to admit his mother to the hospital, so he requested me to drive the truck to Mussoorie. He told me exactly where I needed to go in Mussoorie.

As I was there alone, I agreed. He was really worried about his mother, so I did not say much. He thanked me and left for Delhi. I took the truck and started driving towards Mussoorie. After a while, a van came in front of me. He was driving so slow that I had no option but to overtake him. I honked at him and gave him an indicator that allowed me to give some space to overtake, but god knows why he never let me do it.

After a point, he started to accelerate the van. I also speeded up, then suddenly he stopped and gave me an indicator to overtake. The truck had a problem with the steering wheel. When I tried to steer away, it turned swiftly.

I lost control and hit a car which was coming from the front. After that, my truck collided with a big stone and I didn't see where the car went. I became unconscious.

After sometime when I woke up, I looked for the car and didn't find it anywhere. When I looked down the hill, I saw a car which was broken down. I was scared. There was no one on the road and I quickly started to run away from the site. After running for a few kilometers, I boarded another bus and came back to Mussoorie.

The next day, I saw the picture of the truck I was driving with the headline. *Jagan Thakur died in a car accident. The search is on for the truck driver.*

Then I realized what I had done. Ramesh framed me in the accident by giving me a faulty truck to drive, but I was helpless. I tried to reach out to him, but the phone was not reachable.

After that day, I told Ranjit that my father was ill. I had to go back home and he allowed me. I ran away from Mussoorie. A few months later, the matter was closed and nothing happened. So, I came back here and started to live a regular life. After two years, the investigation opened again.

Looks like someone had seen me there, and now the police have proof that I was driving the truck. It might be Ramesh himself.

•

Shukla took a pause and said, "Tell me what I should do now."

I was silent for a minute and said, "I think you should tell this to Ranjit. He will surely help you."

"I can't tell him anything. Now, I have those bags with me." Shukla said.

"You will come out of it, Shukla."

26
Jay Chandra

The next day, I was at Brajesh's house, watering the plants. I was thinking about my new mobile app VoiceEat. Since I had decided that I would build an app for the phone, this app was always in my mind after the Rubik's cube problem.

While I was thinking about the architectural design of the app, I saw Brajesh coming out of the house to drop someone at the gate. Then he came to me and asked, "How are you feeling now?"

"I am feeling good. The swelling has almost gone," I showed him my hand.

"That's good, Aru. Take care of yourself." Brajesh told me.

I quickly asked Brajesh, "Sir, can I ask you one thing?"

"Yeah, sure."

"How did your father die?"

Brajesh was taken aback by the sudden question, but then told me everything. While narrating the story, he was very calm. It seemed that the pain had subsided.

"Did you find the driver?" I asked him.

"Yes, inspector Vishal, the same person who just left, got some clue about him. Soon, the truck driver will be behind bars." Brajesh smiled and walked inside the house.

I thought that Vishal must have very concrete evidence against Shukla.

After my work at Brajesh's house, I came out of the house, waiting for the diver to drop me to the college in the car.

While I was standing there, I saw Vishal speaking to someone on the phone. He said, "We have to wait till 24th. Ranjit has to make sure that it is out on 23rd anyhow. It can't be delayed. After all, it's because of lord Shiva that everything is happening. *Jai bhole nath!*"

Vishal took a pause and listened. Later he replied, "No Shukla, not now. After 25th. Wait till then!" He hung the phone and came back onto the bike.

When he turned, he saw me standing within earshot. He looked at me and said, "You work at Brajesh's house, right? How is your hand?"

I nodded my head and said, "It is okay now."

He chuckled and said, "Jai bhole nath!"

•

Pandit was planning to go to Delhi to seek more information about Jay. One of his college-mates was posted as an IAS officer. He was calling Pandit for a long time to meet him there.

Pandit thought it would be a good break from what was happening in Mussoorie, since he had reached a dead end in his investigation. He left for Delhi without telling Brajesh because he thought that the trip would not last for more than three days.

Pandit met Shankar in Delhi. Even though he was an IAS officer now, when he met Pandit, there was no protocol. They met just like old friends. Shankar met Pandit at his office and asked him to have dinner at his place that night.

"You were a freelancer in Mumbai when I last met you. Then I remember you had planned to open a startup. You attended some seminars and presentations to pitch the idea to get an investor, but that didn't work. So, what now? Did you get anyone interested in your startup or still looking for someone?"

"I have taken a break from that. Last time we spoke, I told you that I enjoy being an investigator. I also helped Mumbai Police solve some crimes. When I started with them, it was mostly cyber-related stuff, but later, I got some experience in solving murder-related cases also," Pandit said and chuckled.

"That's good Pandit. Why don't you help us? Stay here in Delhi. What are you doing in Mussoorie?" Shankar looked at Pandit.

"In Mussoorie, it's the same work. I am helping to find the truth behind an accident of my school friend's father. My friend Brajesh is very upset about it. He thinks that the police are not doing the job well. Although that incident happened two years ago, he believes that the police have dragged the investigation a lot. By the way, one of the suspects is from Delhi, Jay Chandra. Do you know about him?" Pandit asked.

"Who? That wholesale dealer? He was killed a few weeks back," Shankar told Pandit.

"Killed...? When...?" Pandit asked.

"It has been a few weeks now. He was in his shop and early morning, a few shooters killed him point-blank in his office." Shankar took a pause and continued.

"As fate would have it, those shooters also met with an accident just after they killed Jay," Shankar said.

"Things are going from bad to worse. My next suspect is also gone. It looks like this case will never be solved and one poor innocent guy will die in this game," Pandit.

Shankar asked Pandit to explain what exactly happened. Pandit told the story about the truck driver Shukla and the stolen truck.

"That truck was never stolen. We got to know that he sold the truck to someone in Mussoorie. Later, the guy he sold the truck to, never paid back. So, he reported it as stolen. We got to know this a few days back," Shankar said.

"Jay Chandra sold the truck? That is surprising. Police in Mussoorie thought that it was stolen," Pandit said and asked, "Can I get the details of who he sold the truck to? It's very important for me, Shankar."

Shankar smiled and agreed to help him.

27

VoiceEat

I was now very close to building my app VoiceEat. I worked day and night and requested Trivedi that I won't be able to work in the canteen. He permitted me to stay at home.

One day, Trivedi asked me to come to canteen and take a break from my work. It was after a long time that I went to the canteen. As soon as I reached the canteen, everyone started calling me 'shortcut'. I can never forget that word in my life. Trivedi was surprised. I kept walking, paying no heed to these insults.

On the startup front, I was on the verge of completing the final user interface screen for user login. After the last hurdle was over, I managed to get it through. Finally, I had my first cross-platform app running. Prof Mishra helped me to open an in-app account store so that I could upload the application.

The first video which I uploaded was of that café, where Shukla and I had celebrated Trivedi's birthday. Then, I uploaded my video where I told everyone to come to aunty's cafe.

Next morning, when I woke up, I saw one hundred app downloads in one night. I texted Pandit the screenshot of the application. He was elated that I had developed my first app. Then, he called me.

"Hi Aru, I am really glad to see you growing so fast. Now, I want to tell you something."

"What?" I knew Pandit would tell me about Shukla and how much trouble he was in.

"I was also like you when I developed my first application. Then, I decided to build my startup, my own business. I searched for an investor who could put money in my business. After searching and managing people in my social circle, I found one seminar to pitch my idea to investors. Somehow, I managed to get a pass and attend it. I went through the first two rounds, but in the last round, one of my partners backed out. I was alone in front of them. I lost my confidence and the investor too. I was broken to the extent that I never tried to pitch again. And now, I am working as a detective."

He tried to pep me up. "I want you to present your idea to investors. You now know how to manage a team, since you've been working with your college students. You also have the experience of developing codes and apps. The way you have progressed in a short span of time is incredible. You are very talented, Aru. I am sure you will get someone who can invest money in your idea."

"Can I do that, Pandit?"

"You told me the same thing when I asked you to try your luck at learning programming. Initially, you hesitated and didn't want to do it, but look at yourself now," Pandit replied.

Pandit's words made me more enthusiastic. I said, "Can I meet you to know more about it?"

Pandit said that he was in Delhi to meet his friend. He would also be looking at the truth behind the truck that was stolen from Jay. In a few days, I would finally know what really happened.

In the café, aunty was full of joy. She was serving more customers now. Everyone who visited aunty told her that they came to know the cafe through the VoiceEat app. and a video that featured her and the cafe.

•

One day, while I was walking down the street, I saw that there was a lot of hustle-bustle in the cafe. When I went in, what I saw amazed me. The café was full of customers.

"What happened, aunty? Did you get some magic wand? Such a great crowd," I asked.

"Aru, I also don't know what exactly happened. These people are coming here through an app. They say that the video message was so great that they thought of coming down to taste the cakes. And guess what, they all liked it!" Aunty was shouting and laughing in excitement.

I asked, "Did you see the video?"

"No not yet, I want to see though," she said while serving one customer.

I came out of the café and opened the app dashboard. I could see that there were around 10K views of my video review. I quickly checked the download counter of my app. It had crossed 50K. My app was trending on the charts.

I texted Pandit.

I want to have my own startup, guide me, how can I reach out for that seminar?

Great, Aru. I will send you one link. Start preparing your profile.

When Pandit replied to me, he got a message from Milan.

The date is 23rd of the next month. The cannabis will be in purest form. Shiva agaman will be there.

Pandit calculated that only one month was left for the marijuana to be cut and exported.

•

When I came back home the next day, I saw Shukla in the house. I told him about what I had heard from Vishal outside Brajesh's house. When I told him that story, he panicked. He had only a few days left before any action could be taken against him. He decided that he would leave Mussoorie.

I convinced Shukla to meet Ranjit and tell him what had happened. I promised him that I would save him from Ranjit at any cost.

That night, Shukla took me to Ranjit's house. Ranjit came out in the garden and met us there. He was upset because Rahul's health was deteriorating day by day. On top of it, the other concern was that he would ship marijuana himself this time.

He looked at Shukla and angrily asked, "What happened, Shukla? Don't you think you are late for your confession on the bags that you stole from me? Yesterday, I sent two men to get you, but you were not at your house. But now, it's good that you came here by yourself. Tell me what should I do with you? You know what happens when someone betrays me."

"Please Ranjit sir, you should listen to Shukla's story first and why he did what he did. And there is more that he wants to confess to you," I said.

"Who are you, boy? Are you with him in this?" Ranjit shouted at me.

"I am Aru, Ranjit sir. I am not involved in this, but right now, I am the only one who can give you what you want," I said in a calm voice.

"Don't be stupid. Understand," Ranjit shouted and continued, "I am Ranjit Singhania. People like Shukla, if they think they can betray me and get away with it, then that's not going to happen," Ranjit said in a loud voice.

"After listening to Shukla's story, you decide what you want to do. Then I will speak," I said.

Ranjit looked at Shukla and said, "Tell me everything."

Shukla narrated the whole story to him.

"Shukla, you have ruined me completely. Now I am going to tell Brajesh what you did. I will hand you over to him and then, he will let go of the grudge that he has against me." Ranjit took out the phone and started to look for Brajesh's number.

Shukla looked at me and I said, "Wait, Ranjit sir, wait!"

Ranjit took a pause and looked at me.

"My blood group is AB negative. I have both my kidneys functioning. I can donate one kidney to Rahul. But against that, I want you to save Shukla from Brajesh." I said in a loud voice.

Ranjit disconnected the phone and said, "What did you just say?"

"I can donate my kidney to Rahul," I repeated myself.

"Are you serious?" Ranjit said in a stammering voice.

Shukla looked at me. He held my shoulder and said, "Aru, why are you doing this?"

I looked at Shukla and said, "I promised you, Shukla, I would do whatever it takes to save you."

Then I looked at Ranjit and said, "Did you like the deal, Ranjit? I am ready to donate my kidney if you promise to save Shukla."

Ranjit called his family doctor to verify what I was saying. The doctor took my blood sample and went to the hospital for the result. Shukla and I were waiting in the garden in Ranjit's house. After an hour, the doctor came to share the good news.

"That is true, Ranjit, that is true. This boy's blood group matches Rahul's. We can run a few more tests tomorrow and this boy can donate his kidney to our Rahul."

Ranjit got up and hugged me tightly, "Thank you Aru. You don't know what you are doing for me."

"But I need you to promise me that you will save Shukla from Brajesh," I confirmed.

"It's my promise, Aru. From now onwards, no one can touch Shukla," Ranjit said.

"And one more thing Ranjit. Please treat this as my request… Don't tell Rahul about this," I requested Ranjit.

"But why?"

"Please promise me you won't Rahul," I begged.

Ranjit looked at the doctor and then at me, "Okay, I won't tell him about you."

I thanked Ranjit and told him that I will be in Mussoorie and won't leave this city without telling him. The doctor asked me to visit the hospital soon.

•

When I reached home, I decided to tell everything to Pandit. So, I texted him.

It's urgent; call me when you are free.

Then I opened the laptop and checked my mail. I had been shortlisted to present my business idea to the investors. I was overjoyed.

After a while, Pandit called me up and said, "I got to know what happened with Jay's truck. Someone called Ramesh Tiwari bought the truck from him and never paid the money. And I also know that Ramesh Tiwari works for Bhandari. So there is something big that Bhandari is doing here. I need to find that out."

I chuckled and said, "That's great Pandit! You are close to solve this case. Shukla told me that Ramesh Tiwari gave Shukla the truck that day to drive till Mussoorie. And it was a well-planned attempt by someone to kill Jagan."

I told Shukla's complete story to him.

Pandit said, "We need to talk, Aru. I am coming tomorrow to Mussoorie. I want to meet you both."

Pandit got the information that he was looking for – the truck in Delhi. He wrapped up his visit in Delhi to come back to Mussoorie. He tried to reach out to inform Shankar that he would be leaving for Mussoorie, but Shankar was unavailable. Finally, he called Pandit in the evening.

"Pandit, so you are packing up?" Shankar said.

"Yeah almost," Pandit said.

"I wanted to tell you that we have captured Ramesh Tiwari. He was caught by the Narcotics Control Bureau when he was trying to cross the border to Nepal," Shankar said.

"Ramesh Tiwari is arrested! That is good news, Shankar. He is the key to Jagan's death. Can I meet him?"

"Not now Pandit. He will be in Delhi after two days. Since yesterday night, we have been busy working with the NCB team here. There is some big movement of drug mafia active in India. We have information from a very reliable source that a big consignment will be shipped to Magnolia. Some informers, are saying that it is one of the biggest shipments. The market is speculating that the cost of this shipment is over a billion dollars. The whole department is on fire. Everyone is up on their feet since yesterday night. Ramesh's arrest can reveal some vital clues about it," Shankar said.

"Narcotic Bureau? I know what's going to happen." Pandit replied worried.

"What is going to happen? Do you have any leads? Tell me, Pandit," Shankar asked.

"I will let you know once I get more information. But nothing will happen till 22nd. Whatever will happen, will happen only after 23rd," Pandit said.

28

An Unexpected Twist

I never thought that my time in Mussoorie would give me such life-altering experiences.

That day I called Aai and told her about the app which I had designed and my selection in the seminar. I was so thrilled that I did not leave out any detail. I informed her that I would go to Mumbai in the next few days and be back soon.

"I am very happy that you have achieved a lot in such a small span of time, Aru. Always remember where you started from. Trivedi has done a lot for you. Always be grateful to him. Be humble and honest and never hide anything from me."

"Aai, you know I can't hide anything from you. Please trust me. I will always remember the values that you have inculcated in me."

After speaking with her, I took a deep breath and murmured to myself.

"I hope that she doesn't come to Mussoorie, else it would be very difficult to hide my commitment to Ranjit."

•

Pandit met me at Mussoorie. I took Shukla with me. Shukla told the story about the truck accident, what happened with Jay when he was killed and Ranjit's plan of shipping marijuana.

"We have to keep watching our backs. Something is going to happen after 23rd. Shukla, can we find out why Ranjit is shipping this marijuana?"

"What I know is that he has to do a total of four shipments. Two were completed by me and the rest are left."

"Vishal was saying that he knew Ranjit would have to ship the rest. We need to find out who is shipping the rest," I said.

Shukla said that it was highly confidential. All he could say was that if Ranjit doesn't get anyone then, he would make the third shipment by himself.

Meanwhile, his phone flashed with a message notification. Shukla read and informed us.

"Ranjit is going to Delhi tomorrow, driving the SUV himself. This should surely be the third shipment. Because he never drives himself for such a long journey."

"Why is he doing this?" Pandit asked.

"Why don't we ask him?" I said.

"He won't say anything," Shukla said.

"He will," I said and chuckled.

•

That night we went to Ranjit's house. He was happy to see me. I was his last hope to save Rahul. Pandit and I narrated the complete story to Ranjit and said that we wanted to know about the consignment.

"If you want Rahul's life to be saved, then please tell us the truth," I asserted.

Ranjit said, "Jagan was a good soul. He always helped people. Even though he was in the timber business, he still helped in forest preservation and worked with NGOs to save it. One day, he discovered that the land area inside the forest was full of marijuana. It grew in the jungle by itself. He decided that he would let the government know about this.

"On the personal front, Jagan was struggling to repay the loan he had taken for his business. The loan amount was huge; even I couldn't have helped him. It was tough for him to pay that off. But then, Bhandari came into the picture. He told Jagan that if he could ship four harvests of marijuana to a Mongolian syndicate, they would pay off his debt. He came to me for seeking advice. Initially, I told Jagan not to do this, since it was illegal. But frankly, we had no choice.

"So, Jagan and I decided that he would agree to four harvests and after that, we would inform the government about it. That way, further illegal shipment of drugs would happen. Jagan and I met with his Mongolian client. He agreed to the deal and Jagan was paid in full at the same time. He was out of debt the very next day. But after that, a few weeks later, Shukla's truck hit Jagan's car. He fell off the cliff and died.

"Later, I received a call from this Mongolian client where he told me that he did not need the harvest at that time, but he would need it in the next two years. He gave me a few dates to arrange for the shipment. I had no option but to deliver what Jagan had promised. Else they would have come after me and Rahul. I didn't tell this to Brajesh because I didn't want him to meet these syndicates and fall into a trap like we did."

"When is the last day of the harvest?"

"On the 23rd, they were very adamant that I should cut the harvest on the 23rd only. This is my last shipment and then, I will be free."

"Thanks, Ranjit! Now I will tell you the truth. Jagan was not killed by Shukla's truck. He was murdered by someone just after the accident. And that field is cursed. After the last harvest, someone close to you will die. And I know that Rahul is not well these days," Pandit told Ranjit.

Pandit said that he needed to meet the fruit seller Ram Kumar and alert him to be safe because he was the only one who had seen how Jagan was murdered.

•

There was a lot happening in my life. On the professional front, I had to pitch my business idea to an investor which would change my life forever. And on the personal front, I had to go through a medical check-up so that I could donate my kidney to Rahul.

So in a single day, my life would take an unexpected turn. Who knew what was waiting for me!

•

When I reached Mumbai, the total download of VoiceEat had reached two-hundred thousand. Now, I had a solid case to present to investors.

I had a fantastic day at the seminar. They loved the way I talked about myself and presented my app VoiceEat. Whatever English I had learned in my speaking course came to my rescue. When I reached the stage to talk about my ambition and newly developed application VoiceEat, I wasn't hesitant. I remembered the day Andre had called me up on the stage. But that grudge against him gave me more courage to climb up the stairs with pride. I knew I had *not* taken a shortcut. Andre's words echoed in my mind. *Be a lion!*

The appreciation which I received from the audience really sparked my spirits. Eventually, I reached the final round. If I managed to impress the judges, I could get the investment of around one million dollars.

After the event, I came back to Mussoorie that night itself. The next day, I got a message from Pandit that the fruit seller is dead. He met with an accident while coming back home a few days back. It was very evident that it was murder. And there was now no evidence to show that Shukla was innocent. Meanwhile, I went to the hospital to get my medical tests done.

Ranjit was under immense pressure to deliver the third assignment. He decided to deliver it himself. So he planned to deliver the consignment at the earliest.

The next day, he drove to Delhi with the bag. This time, he was received by the member of the Mongolian syndicate who came to collect the consignment. Ranjit met him at The Leela Palace hotel.

He reached the hotel and waited for him at the café. The syndicate member entered and extended his hand. "Hi Ranjit! Nice to meet you. I am Qadan. Nice to see you. I never expected that you will come yourself to deliver the consignment."

"It's the fourth and the final one, Qadan. After that, no more commitment!" Ranjit said.

"Don't worry, I have to ensure that the final one is the purest. I can't take any risks," Qadan said. He continued, "So, I will be there with my tester to test the sample before we pack the consignment."

"I am not responsible for the purity Qadan. You have a commitment to Bhandari. This is between you and him," Ranjit said.

"Yes, I know Ranjit. So Bhandari and I will be there at your small, made-up village. I would also like to be blessed by lord Shiva," Qadan chuckled.

"Lord Shiva will never bless you," Ranjit said and walked out of the café. Later, he drove back to Mussoorie.

Brajesh was waiting for Vishal to give him some progress, so he called him. As Vishal entered, Brajesh asked, "What is the news, Vishal? Can we get Ranjit?" he said anxiously.

"Yes, we are almost there,"Vishal said.

"You have been telling me this since last week. You have a convict in front of you, walking freely, and you can't even arrest him," Brajesh said in a loud voice.

"We can't make any arrests unless we have any solid evidence, Brajesh."

"Get Shukla into custody and interrogate him. He will spill everything."

"It doesn't work that way, Brajesh."

"Suddenly you seem helpless to me, Vishal. What happened?" Brajesh asked angrily.

"Nothing, we are doing the investigation properly."

"Or you have also sold yourself to Ranjit? Tell me," Brajesh shouted.

"Brajesh, please don't say that. Let me tell you this. Shukla is protected by Ranjit now, and the only eye witness that we had is dead. So I don't have to tell you who did that," Vishal replied in anger.

"Ranjit...! Now, I have to deal with Ranjit personally," Brajesh said.

"Don't do anything Brajesh. We will handle it," Vishal said.

"You do your work Vishal. I don't trust anyone. Let the police do their work and I will do mine," Brajesh said and asked him to go.

Vishal came out and dialled Bhandari's number.

"I told him that the eye witness is dead. I shouldn't have told him now. I should have waited till 23rd. My mistake!"

•

Finally, I received a call from the investors that they were happy to put money in my startup. My happiness knew no bounds. My eyes were brimming with tears of joy. But that happiness lasted for a few minutes. I got a call from Ranjit that he wanted to meet me in his house and the medical report had come. Shukla knew what I had committed to Ranjit. And Trivedi was baffled to see the sudden change in my expression.

While I left, Trivedi asked Shukla, "What happened, Shukla? He was called all of a sudden. Is there any problem?"

Shukla told Trivedi everything, who was shocked to hear what I had committed to Ranjit to save Shukla's life. But it was much more than that. The life of many people was impacted by my decision. I was not only saving Shukla's life, but also saving Ranjit and Rahul. And of course, that girl's happiness mattered a lot to me.

I reached Ranjit's house. The report saddened him. He called me inside the room and said, "Aru, I have got your report. Do you want to know what's there?"

"Yes. What's the issue? I can donate the kidney, right?" I asked him.

"Yes, you can, but out of your two kidneys, one is small and dysfunction so that can't be taken out. It is very weak. So I want to ask you, will you donate the good one?" Ranjit said.

"Yes Ranjit, I will. I know what I am doing." I smiled.

"But you can't survive for too long, with the other kidney, Aru. So it's almost as if you will be giving your life to Rahul."

"I understand, Ranjit. But this decision is not only impacting Rahul's life. There are many others who will be positively impacted with my choice. So, yes, I will donate it to Rahul. I have to sign an offer from an investor for my startup. For that, I will go to Mumbai for a day tomorrow. I want to enjoy this moment, Ranjit," I said.

Suddenly, a loud noise was heard outside the house. We both stood up and looked outside. Brajesh stepped out of his BMW.

He came shouting, "Ranjit, come out!"

Ranjit was astonished at what was happening in front of his eyes. Brijesh was holding a gun.

Brajesh came in and he looked at me and said, "Aru, you…" Then, he looked at Ranjit and shouted, "You killed my Pa and now you are eliminating all the eyewitnesses. I know Shukla is under your protection, but he will not be spared."

"Listen to me, Brajesh sir. That's not the truth," I said.

"You go away, Aru. I need to sort this out today," Brajesh shouted.

"Wait Brajesh, listen to me," Ranjit said.

"It's over now, Ranjit. I am done. I am frustrated with the legal process. I will deliver justice now," Brajesh shouted in anger at Ranjit.

"Brajesh sir, listen to him please," I shouted.

"Aru you go!" Brajesh shouted

"No, I will not go. You keep the gun down first," I shouted.

"Listen to me Brajesh," Ranjit shouted.

Brajesh was in no mood to listen to Ranjit. He pointed his pistol at Ranjit and fired two shots in his abdomen. He instantly started to bleed.

I ran towards Brajesh and took his gun and said, "You go away, Brajesh! I don't have anything to lose here. I will say I have killed him." Then, I started to run out of the house with the gun.

Brajesh shouted: "Wait, Aru wait…"

All the servants and guards rushed inside after listening to the gunshot. While they were running inside, they saw me running out of the house with the gun. They thought that I had shot Ranjit and immediately called the police.

Without wasting even a single minute, I came home. Shukla was at home and I asked him to drive me out of Mussoorie. I needed to reach Mumbai at the earliest.

Shukla started the SUV that he had parked outside of the house and drove me out. The police came to my house within a few minutes and got to know I was leaving Mussoorie. They came after us.

Within a few minutes, we were on the highway to Delhi. I called Pandit and told him what had happened at Ranjit's house. I asked him if he could book my ticket to Mumbai from Delhi tonight. Pandit was shocked to know how events had unfolded.

When Pandit reached Ranjit's house, he saw an ambulance taking Ranjit out on a stretcher to the hospital. Brajesh was there, standing near the ambulance. Pandit reached Brajesh and pulled him aside. He looked at him and then, to the ambulance.

"What have you done, Brajesh? Do you know what Ranjit has done for you?"

Pandit explained to Brajesh what happened with Jagan and it was not Shukla but someone else who killed him. He told him about me and how I had saved Shukla from Ranjit's anger.

"Poor Aru! On one hand, his dreams are coming true, but on the other hand, he is donating his kidney and is on the verge of getting caught by police who is chasing him for Ranjit's murder," Pandit said in anguish.

Brajesh was deeply shocked. He said, "No matter what happens, I will save Aru."

Then, Pandit received a call from Shankar.

"Ramesh Tiwari confessed to the murder of Jagan. He was the one in the van which killed Jagan."

"But he left that place after giving the truck to Shukla. How did he come into the van?" Pandit asked.

"He left the place and came back again in the van. Bhandari is behind all this. He is the one who trapped Ranjit in shipping the marijuana from that land. I want to catch him red-handed so we are coming on 23rd" Shankar said.

Pandit agreed with Shankar and hung up. He looked at Brajesh and said, "We found Jagan uncle's killer. But please don't do anything now. There is a big syndicate behind all this. Just wait till 23rd."

"Who is the killer?" Brajesh begged in front of Pandit.

"Bhandari," Pandit replied.

Brajesh was deeply shattered upon realizing what he had done. Pandit said, "It is our duty to save Ranjit."

When the ambulance left, a servant came out and said, "Rahul Baba has fainted, please call the ambulance."

•

While Brajesh admitted Rahul to the hospital, Pandit was also with him. He told Pandit that on the last harvest, he wanted to finish the last consignment by himself. Pandit said that it was cursed and whoever takes it from the fields is destined to suffer.

Brajesh said that it would not be him but Bhandari who would cut the final harvest. Pandit didn't understand how that would happen. Leaving Ranjit and Rahul in the hospital, Brajesh asked Pandit to come home where they would make a plan to trap Bhandari.

•

On 23rd, Pandit set out for the forest. While they reached the small aloof village where marijuana was being packed, the sky slowly turned red. As they went close to the field, they saw that every plant in the field was drenched in red. The red colour light was getting emitted from the temple. It was the same scene as described in the palm leaf manuscript. Pandit and Brajesh looked at each other and said, "Hey bhole nath, bless us."

Brajesh told the villagers that they must not cut the harvest as Ranjit was not there and there was no instruction from him. Pandit and Brajesh waited for Bhandari to come.

Pandit informed Shankar that he was already in the field. He told Shankar to follow his GPS location and reach there as soon as he could. After a while, Bhandari came, walking down the path. There was a group of bodyguards with him, along with Qadan. When he reached the village, he saw that the men had stopped working. He said, "What are you waiting for?"

Then, Pandit and Brajesh came out to confront Bhandari. Brajesh looked at him angrily. Pandit kept holding Brajesh's hand so that he could keep him in control.

Bhandari was surprised, "Where is Ranjit? He has to fulfill his commitment for the final consignment, which your dead father had asked him to do." He chuckled.

Brajesh moved to hit Bhandari, but Pandit pulled him back.

Pandit said, "Ranjit is in ICU so unless these villagers don't get an order to cut the harvest, they won't cut it."

Bhandari chuckled, "And now you want *me* to ask them to cut it so that I get the curse of lord Shiva. Forget about it."

Qadan was listening to Bhandari and said, "Bhandari, I don't have much time. You better ask them to start cutting the harvest." The sky was completely red now and everyone knew that lord Shiva had descended. They knew the field had got the gold they were looking for.

Bhandari was adamant that he won't give the instruction to cut the crop.

Qadan went to Bhandari and said, "I don't want to go empty-handed. The whole world is waiting for this."

Bhandari was terrified by Qadan, so he shouted at the villagers and ordered them. Pandit and Brajesh smirked. Bhandari shouted in frustration to Pandit and Brajesh, "I gave them the order, but you guys will not go alive from here."

Pandit and Brajesh laughed.

Bhandari ordered the villagers to cut the harvest. He took out his pistol and pointed at both of them. The villagers went inside the field to cut the harvest.

Shankar came inside the village and covered Bhandari and Qadan and asked them to surrender.

Suddenly, Bhandari's bodyguard shot at the police. To counter them, the police responded back. In a few seconds, heavy gunfire started. The villagers were still cutting the harvest. Qadan told them not to stop. Whenever villagers cut the fruit, it bled in red. Heavy exchange of fire between the police and Bhandari continued.

•

In Mumbai, I went inside the building where I needed to meet the investors. After all the formalities, when I was coming out, I got a message from Pandit's friend.

The police is outside the main gate of your building. They are looking for you. Come from the back side.

I rushed out from the back side where Pandit's friend was standing with a car. I swiftly went in and we drove directly to the airport. The police came to know that I had left the building so they also came back, following us. I went to the airport and boarded the flight. But, the police thought that I was still in Mumbai, hiding somewhere.

In Mussoorie, I got to know that Rahul had fainted and was admitted to the hospital. Ranjit was also in the ICU. Somehow, I dodged the police at Delhi airport, reached Mussoorie and then the hospital so that I could donate my kidney and fulfill my promise.

Finally, I reached the room where Ranjit was admitted I looked at him and murmured, "I am here, Ranjit. Don't worry. Rahul will be alright."

I went to the room where Rahul was admitted. But, I was surprised to see that he was not in his bed. I asked the nurse what happened. The nurse said that Rahul was being operated on. My heartbeat increased and I started to pray for Rahul's safety. I asked her why he was in the operation theatre. She said that a donor had come in today, looking for Rahul. I asked her who the donor was, to which she replied, a lady in her late fifties. I was happy that Rahul was safe, but was surprised thinking who this donor could be with this rare blood group.

•

After the long encounter between Bhandari, Qadan and the police force, they were captured. The villagers also cut the harvest and came out. The police arrested Bhandari and Qadan with five hundred kilograms of marijuana. The syndicate was also caught that night. When the police measured the quality of it, it was in the purest form.

Pandit and Brajesh came running to the hospital. They saw me. I was standing outside of the operation theater. I saw Trivedi and Shukla coming to me. I was surprised to see them there. Then Pandit and Brajesh came to me and asked where Rahul was.

I said, "He is being operated. Some old lady donated her kidney to him. I am standing here to see who she is."

One nurse came to Brajesh saying that Ranjit was out of danger. He would be discharged soon.

Trivedi and Shukla came and hugged me. But they were looking sad. I was anxious to know what had happened.

I asked, "Trivedi, what happened? Why are you guys so worried? Tell me, is Rahul okay?"

Trivedi held my hand and said, "I told everything about you to your Aai, Aru. She came here to Mussoorie."

I smiled, "Aai is here? Wow, where is she? Let's go home and meet her."

Trivedi said, "She is here, Aru. She is the one who gave her kidney to Rahul. The operation is successful; the doctors are waiting for both of them to get stable. After that, both of them will be discharged."

Then, the gate of the operation theatre opened. I could see Aai on the stretcher, with an oxygen mask on. She was unconscious.

"Your Aai is an embodiment of god," Brajesh kept his hand on my shoulder and told me. I stood there motionless. Tears were rolling down my cheeks.

Later, I saw that girl who was rushing inside the operation theater. She went in and looked at Rahul.

"I told you I will be fine!" Rahul said and smiled.

A couple of days later, Ranjit also came out from the ICU. I left Mussoorie with Aai to start my new life– as A.I., in Mumbai.

Epilogue

There was absolue silence as Arvind finished his speech. The audience was mesmerized by his success story.

The application VoiceEat had more than ten million downloads now. Gradually, he had managed to expand by opening his office in all major cities in India. Recently his company had signed a multi-million-dollar deal with a US Pharma company.

From a canteen boy to A.I., Arvind's journey was an epitome of relentless hardwork and commitment to excellence.

Everyone stood up and gave him a standing ovation.

Arvind gazed across the auditorium and then, looking up, he thanked his Aai who had passed away an year ago. She was lucky enough to see him evolve and grow into an established entrepreneur.

"Thanks, Arvind. Thanks to A.I., for his amazing inspirational story. I am sure everyone can feel the goose bumps. I am feeling it too! We can learn a lot from you, Arvind. With that golden speech by the great man himself, let us now welcome on stage, Geeta Singhania from Mussoorie. She will be enlightening us about the art of living and loving."

While walking out of the auditorium, he heard the words 'Mussoorie' and 'Singhania'. Out of curiosity, he turned back and looked at the poster where the name and picture of speakers were mentioned.

Finally, he saw the *same* girl smiling at him. The girl who didn't have a name until now.